Books by NIKOLA STEFAN (including Upcoming)

Tale of Tales – Part I[1] – A Strange Bunch

Tale of Tales – Part II[2] – The Witch-borne Quests

Tale of Tales – Part III[3] – Familiars and Foes

Watch for more at www.NikolaStefan.com
& follow AuthorNikolaStefan on Facebook

---

[1] www.nikolastefan.com/book/tale-of-tales-part-1

[2] www.nikolastefan.com/book/tale-of-tales-part-2

[3] www.nikolastefan.com/book/tale-of-tales-part-3

TALE of TALES

Part I: A Strange Bunch

Nikola Stefan

Tale of Tales – Part I – A Strange Bunch

ISBN (Paperback): 978-86-6138-001-3

Latest on Vitor: www.Linktr.ee/VitorPublishing

A Word from the Author: Subscribe to my infrequent newsletter, featuring book-release dates and a chance of an Advance Review Copy, at: www.NikolaStefan.com/Subscribe

Dedication

To nameless bards and storytellers whose words have been my guideposts.

Contents

OPENING NOTES

THERE ARE MANY MYTHICAL BEINGS IN THIS BOOK that are unknown in English and most other languages. It was a great endeavor to make them all conceivable. A good example is *dragon,* as there are three types: the *fiery dragon* is a huge reptile with wings, a being that carries a fire inside him, as known in English. But, there is also a human form that is his descendant and ascendant, a human with great power, usually called *dragonkin,* some of which can even shapeshift into a dragon-like form and fly. The third form is the *spirit dragon,* the most unusual and most powerful of them all – this invisible essence willingly resides only in a special human, called a *zduhač,* who is unable to control it, and it is the only being that is able to confront *ala,* the ancient beast that brings havoc upon men; when ala strikes, the spirit dragon leaves its transient vessel, the body of the zduhač, to fight its archenemy in the sky. The reader should not be confused when any of these three forms of dragon (*fiery dragon, dragonkin,* or *spirit dragon*) are referred to simply as: dragon. In general, all mythical beings are explained through tales or dialogues before or after they first appear.

When the gods are mentioned, the capital letter is reserved only for the supreme God, the asleep Creator who dreams the universe and everything in it into being, thus the Father of all other *gods*.

On spelling: When a double-sign is used up above the letter in the folklore-spelling of names and titles, like *zduhač* mentioned above, a reader need to imagine "h" after that character and read these two letters as a single hard voice they become. Therefore, Miloš is Milosh, Baš Čelik is pronounced as Bash Chelik, and Žarko reads as Zharko (similar to the beginning sound of the French-derived word *gendarme* or to the voice "s" in *measure*). In contrast, a single line above the letter, like in Perunović, means the softer version of the same voice, like the "ch" in *chirping* of birds, or the soft opening sound of *ciao* in Italian, pronounced with tongue touching the front teeth.

On strange namings: The men of Morlak call themselves *Morlaks,* though most outlanders would likely call them *Morlakians*. This chronicle tries its best to respect the locals' ways.

Prologue: The Third Night

The woman beside the stream was visibly worried. Her old, wrinkled face, worn beyond her years, looked weary as she pulled a few pebbles from the bottom of the stream and tossed them into her wooden trough. Despite doing everything in her power, the young, cared-for woman who had recently given birth was not getting any better. Though the red thread tied around the newborn's hand had seemengly helped the baby, the red wool she had tucked behind the ear of the young woman had not helped her recover. And nothing else she had tried had helped the new mother either. Not the garlic hung at the door, nor the stones taken from flowing water, brimming with spirits, which she had each day tossed into the trough after washing the mother's and newborn's clothes. Nor had it helped that, from the time she had given birth, neither the mother nor the child had left the house. Not even that the worried father, at the old woman's insistence, had refused to carry embers from the hearth to rekindle a fire for the nearest neighbour, who had just returned to his lot after being away on trade for several days; no, during those first, perilous days, when various demons lurked before the house, waiting for any opportunity to prey on the mother and newborn, the living fire must not be taken out of the home's heart.

"At least everything seems all right with the child now," she thought. Many of the protective measures she had carried out had been for the sake of the child, and at least these had shown some success. The woman glanced up at the sky for a moment; evening was approaching and she would have to hurry to bring the freshly washed garments of the two unprotected souls back home before darkness set in. She shivered briefly at the very thought of what might happen if the swaddling cloths were to be left outside overnight... No, they had already been through enough misfortune.

"Tonight is the third night," thought the woman as she hastened toward the house. "Everything ought to be resolved tonight, for better or worse." Earlier she had already set out the table inside, with bread, cheese, honey, and even a glass of wine against which she had leaned a silver coin. The offerings were, therefore, ready. As soon as she entered the house, the old woman dressed the child in the father's white shirt and then woke up the mother, who was hovering between dream and reality, still in the grip of the fever that had not left her. Tonight, even this tormented woman, especially this woman, had to stay awake. The future of her newborn child might very well depend on it.

✲✲✲

The mother twitched restlessly. She had fallen asleep! Suddenly she opened her eyes in a panic and took in the scene in front of her – beside the cradle, roughly hewn out of a large chunk of wood, stood three women wearing long white flowing dresses. The Fates! Oh gods! The triad was already here?! How could she have fallen asleep, how could she have let herself, before their arrival?! The three strikingly similar women were poised one next to the other, staring down at the cradle from which the child – or was it just the mother's imagination – returned their gaze with wide-open eyes, completely calmly and quietly. Despite the similarity in the women, the mother had a sense that they were in fact different ages. She wanted to say something to them, to excuse herself, but the guests behaved as if she wasn't even there. And just then, the one who appeared the oldest spoke.

To lose everything, and remain apart, darkness always round her, darkness in her heart! The oldest woman uttered these words with a note of pure malice in her voice, continuing to gaze down directly at the child.

The mother burst out in muffled sobbing with a cry, "No, no, no…" In that terrible instant she was certain that she, because of her negligence, was solely guilty for such a fate. Her child had not been safeguarded through a third night! After a significant lull, the oldest woman turned away from the child, and the middle one began to speak.

To wander the world, without peace or cheer, shadow ever pursuing, and escape nowhere! The voice of the second woman was like the first - perhaps less malevolent, but equally ruthless. The mother was now openly weeping, her heart pierced by these sudden arrows of despair. "No, nooo!" she screamed, but the three women in white continued to disregard her. Just as she herself failed to notice neither the aged hand of the woman wiping her hot face with a wet cloth, nor the worried faces around her. The young mother's ravings were disturbing to the caring old woman and the man who stood off to the side, unsure of what he should do. In the meantime, in the same place, which now seemed as if it belonged to another world, the second woman also turned away from the child in the cradle.

Then the youngest and most beautiful of the three

women spoke up; her voice echoed with a certain care and gentleness that was lacking from the similar, yet distantly cold voices of the elder two. As opposed to them, this youngest woman addressed the child directly, and her words resounded like a lullaby; and truly, the child fell asleep without a sound just as the woman voiced her final words.

Young girl, endure, evil takes its toll, through it all you will emerge with naught, yet pure in soul. And though shadow may threaten all that you hold dear, it cannot possess you, nor the beauty that you bear… At the end of your dark journey you still will feel the light; out of shadows, a whole empire, kingdom beyond sight.

Having uttered these final words, the third woman also turned away, and the three departed without a single step.

✲✲✲

The young mother was now raving incoherently, losing herself often, again and again, and to the old caregiver woman it was becoming clear that perhaps, by the will of those who decide our miserable fates which we struggle against, this tormented soul might not make it through the night. "No… thank you… my thanks… Senka!* Senka… beauty… evil! Evil threatens!" Then there followed a string of disconnected words which neither the old woman nor the worried husband could make sense of. Unfortunately, these words were also her last. As the final fragments foundered from her tongue, her spirit gave way, leaving the newborn child to the mercy of the cruel fate bestowed upon her, and the father to struggle on alone in the world. She had passed, as it had been fated so, and from fate one cannot escape...

With tears brimming in his eyes, which he managed to control only with great effort, the father broke the deathly silence that had seized this home: "My love, go in peace. I shall care for our Senka more than for myself." The aged woman turned to him with surprise, "But the godfather, he has yet to choose a name..." and then she fell silent. The man's look said it all. "The child will be called Senka. That was her mother's dying wish."

*In traditional folklore, the female name *Senka* has the same meaning as the word *shadow*, and remains in usage, though infrequently, as a name today.

– Chapter I –
Senka and Vidra

Senka was happy. It is not hard to be happy when you know so little. She could not know, as no one else could have, that her name was born out of a strange misunderstanding in the thick of a tragedy, but had firmly gripped her father's story that her name was the last wish of her departed mother, the most important gift that she had left her with. In truth, the girl wished for her mother everyday, but this was only a vague desire for something not truly known, which could never be called suffering. She had a father whom she loved, who never raised his hands against her. Even the stepmother rarely beat her, and only when she truly made a mess of things and her father was not there.

From Senka's point of view, life was far from bad. In her twelve years she had developed a heartfelt love for all that was around her. Apart from her father, she felt a deep love for her sister. Truly her half-sister, but Senka never thought of her in such a way, and she would not even have known what "half-sister" meant had her stepmother not used the word often when speaking to her own daughter about Senka. No, she was the one sister Senka had, and she loved her fully. And she never really cared that most of the household chores and disciplining was reserved for her, while her sister received all the love that her "half-mother" was able to offer (Senka laughed out loud the first time she realized that she thought of her stepmother as a half-mother, the "half" part a term that she had no doubt learned from her). She never worried about this lack of love which her stepmother made sure to show everyday – Senka may not have loved her, but she did not hate her either. She understood that her father needed a wife, as everyone needs someone to warm them in their bed; also, there was much woman's work that needed to be done around the house, and Senka was still too young for most of it. She was completely satisfied with the kindness and affection her father showed to her, the endless care that she could see as love. In her father's presence, even this half-mother was nearly pleasant to her. "I may even be getting more love from my father than my sister does," thought Senka, "so it is fine that I am loved less by my half-mother. After all, as strict as she is with me, my father is just as strict with her! And if my mother were alive, surely she would love me more than my sister." And so, finding all these necessary justifications in herself, Senka managed to live life without bitterness.

A great deal of Senka's seemingly unlimited love was reserved for Vidra. Vidra was her dog, her devoted companion since the day she found him in the woods as a puppy, completely wet from tumbling through the stream. "Little Vidra,* so what are you doing there?" Senka asked through laughter, and from the wagging of the pup's little tail, she knew that she had chosen the right name. Her father laughed when he heard it, confirming that she could keep the little male puppy "with a woman's name," but only if nobody came looking for the pup, and on that day there was no happier girl in the world than Senka. So it was… and now, more than three years later, they were still inseparable, the girl and Vidra.

✲✲✲

"Vidra!" shouted Senka, coming back from her thoughts. "Now where is that dog?!" she pondered, "when he was here a moment ago?" Usually, Vidra would stay just to her right when they went to fetch water. Every now and then, she would try to confuse him, moving a step faster, then a step slower as they approached the stream. The dog would handle such games without a hint of effort, rather gracefully, succeeding always in not falling behind nor getting ahead. Senka even had the impression that Vidra would somehow always manage to run along at an even pace – she could never quite figure out how her dog managed to do so, and she loved him all the more for it.

Now the stream was already in sight: Senka had just passed between the two large trees that marked the end of the forest path (if one could call that narrow trail, occasionally trodden by Vidra and Senka, a path at all) and stepped out onto the small clearing in the forest glen. She was expecting to find Vidra, as she sometimes did, happily splashing about in the creek or slurping up water from the stream side. But that was not the case this time.

She stopped and looked around. The dog was indeed standing nearby, but was not looking at her, nor at the stream, but had already climbed up on the rise in the clearing, as if he was struggling to see something in the distance. Whatever it was, it lay in the direction from which they had come, and Senka immediately sensed the tension of her pet – such a thing did not happen often, so she was able to recognize the complete loss of the dog's attention, the elongated ears which in such moments seemed to be larger than they really were, tilted slightly, and the barely noticeable raising of the dog's hair. For a moment she looked back to the safety of the dark forest, then ran to Vidra, leaving the forest behind her, and peered out, following the direction of the dog's gaze. From somewhere behind them, perhaps only a half-hour away, the time they needed for walking to the stream, a thick smoke was rising above the forest.

*In traditional folklore, the female name *Vidra* has the same meaning as the word *otter*.

– Chapter 2 –

The Flames of Change

The scurry through the woods, that followed immediately, Senka would remember as only a blur of incomplete images; several scratches from thorns and branches, a slight tear in the sleeve of her white shirt, her scarf snared by a low stick that dragged it off her head, leaving it hanging from the knotted braid underneath her disheveled hair as she ran on in a panic. Her dog racing by her side, his ears constantly pricked up and his head unnaturally raised, as if any moment they would come across something terrible. An awareness of her right hand pulling back the greenish scarf to the top of her scalp, her left arm reaching for a moment to help, and in this moment the feeling that the empty skin for water was weighing on her more than it ever had before when full. The instant when, breathless, but too frightened to notice her breathlessness, she stopped upon the exit from the forest and, in front of her, saw all that her family possessed. The small field her father toiled over everyday, and the path that led through the field to a small low house made up of a single large room where she had spent most of her life, with its floor of well-pressed earth and hearth in the middle. The moment in which the empty waterskin just dropped from her hand. The next moment in which she again began to run, this time directly to the raging fire devouring what just a short hour before she had called home.

The flame had already engulfed the wooden roof, underneath which lay stores of straw to hold the house's warmth during the cold nights. No one was there to put out the fire; no one was in front of the house. Suprisingly clearheaded, Senka remembered the three large straw mattresses; one on which her father and stepmother slept, another which she shared with her sister, and a third one which was generally empty, intended for expected and unexpected guests alike, who could always assume, as was fitting, that they would be welcomed with hospitality. The wooden table, the wood chairs, stacks of firewood, linen curtains in wooden frames that served in place of walls... their home had been an unlit torch which was now ignited. But, how? To Senka it seemed that, along with the wooden walls, the flame was consuming even the stone foundations which had measured her growing up (the day when she had realized that the stones no longer reached even up to her waist she still remembered fondly); maybe the flames were licking at the old straw, mixed with mud, which had been pushed into the cracks between rocks to keep the weather outside? Or maybe that was just the impression made on her by the fire which now pulsed everywhere through the window frames, those familiar frames small enough so that not too much heat would escape when the wooden shutters were closed, yet large enough to let daylight into the house. A house which was no more.

Senka tried to rush through the door, but was stopped by the heat and the sharp tongues of the flame. The interior of the house looked like a fireplace ablaze – from the intense glow one could no longer see what the fire was feeding upon. The brightness of the blaze forced her to squint and flinch, falling back, her nostrils filled with hot smoke and her eyes with tears. Unaware of her actions, she instinctively ran around the house, trying to look through the window holes, to glimpse anything other than the fiery whips she had faced at the door. But the flames were everywhere, and only flames. Senka realized that she was crying, but she did not know if this was merely because of the fire and smoke. Inside her, she felt nothing but horror:

when she went for water, all had been at home. Her father, stepmother, and sister. She could still clearly see them when she closed her eyes, as if they were still inside the house, somehow mysteriously frozen in a frame of fire: her father sitting at the table, on a long bench that wobbled slightly, after a laborious morning in the fields, drinking from a small wooden cup filled from a similarly rustic jug scratched by years and hands and falls; her stepmother preparing some meal in the small pot hanging above the fireplace, whose color on the bottom had completely worn away; and her sister... Her sister! Panic seized Senka in its cold hands. A chill shivered through her body despite the heat thrown off by the house enveloped in flames. Where are they?

Through her unconscious sobs and cries as she was helplessly running around the house in broken circles, suddenly it seemed to Senka that she heard a muffled shout: "Help!" It was uttered by an unrecognizable voice partially lost in the noise of the crackling wood splintering in the fire. She bounded back to the doorframe and pressed as close she could to the open door. The door itself was as well on fire, even though it still hung firmly, though now pointlessly, to its hinges, rocking back and forth under the pressure of the billowing smoke as the flames went in and out. But behind the door, Senka could finally see that the fire had not yet engulfed the whole hut: just beyond the house threshold, whose wooden beams were also burning, there was a small piece of beaten earth which the fire had not managed to consume. And on that island in a sea of flames lay a snake.

"The House-guardian!" thought Senka immediately. She knew, of course, the story of the snake that watched over the house, ensuring good fortune to the household; she knew that it lived under the house foundations, and that one should never hurt this creature. She had heard all of this, but had never thought about it much; she had never seen such a snake, and neither had her father, though it was he who had spoken of it, saying that it was not at all a bad thing that they had never seen the snake, since its appearance would be an ill omen. Her father could not even describe the snake to her: was it large or small, colorful or not, dangerous or harmless? How had the snake come to live here, what did it eat?... In a world overflowing with visible wonders, Senka never thought too much of the invisible. However, knowing this story, she was now certain of what lay before her.

Without a moment's hesitation, Senka turned and ran to the edge of the field, where her father usually stacked together small piles of hay with a long-handled wooden pitchfork. Senka grabbed the tool and ran back to the house, lowering the spikes of the fork to the ground in front of the snake, pushing it forward through the flames while simultaneously raising her arms as best she could, so that the long handle remained as far as possible from the range of the licking flames. As if by command, the snake immediately crawled onto the pitchfork, quickly wrapped itself around the handle, and with almost unbelievable deftness began slithering upward. Senka lifted the tool and pulled it out of the fire, taking a few steps back from the hungering flame, when she realized with terror that the snake had already managed to reach the top of the handle. Now it had crossed onto her hand! Senka threw down the pitchfork quickly, but too late – the snake had wound itself around her arm! In a flash, she saw the flick of a hornlike tail as it whipped through the air before firmly grasping her wrist, continuing to spiral upwards with the rest of its body, and in the next moment she felt the cold scaly skin of the snake at her throat. Senka shook her head forcefully, but again in vain, for the snake was already wrapped around her neck. The snake's tail now passed over her eyes, touching them as she blinked!

"I save you, and this is your thanks?" Senka murmured in tearful voice, frozen in fear. In a sudden instance of dread, she was sure that the snake was going to strangle her. She lifted her arms in an attempt to tear off the intruder wrapped around her neck, but beneath her fingers, instead of the cold and scaly skin of the snake, she felt the even colder touch of unmoving metal. It had the smoothness of silk, a feel she knew well, having had the chance to touch this delicate fiber often, on the threading of her shawl, despite the meager means of her family. Then, through her confusion, it seemed to her that she heard a rasping, sinuous whisper, as if spoken directly into her ear: "To reccceive, you mussst lose. All are dead. Essscape. If they have not found you, they have sssensssed you. Essscape." It seemed then that the fire dimmed and faded, and around Senka, all fell into darkness.

– Chapter 3 –
A Shadow in the Dark

If the previous events remained only a series of disrupted images for Senka, then the following moments remained an echo of vague noises utterly drowned in a dark sea of unspeakable horror. How could one describe what was happening in the soul of a twelve-year-old girl who was suddenly without her family, without her home, and without sight? For Senka was suddenly blind!

The girl did not immediately realize her loss of sight. For a moment, she thought that she had simply fainted, as happened from time to time; then she thought that it had somehow quickly become night, that everything had just been a nightmare, and that she was safe and sound in the darkness of her own home, wrapped in a swathe of warm blankets, while her sister slept to her right, warming her body. Darkness? The flame in the fireplace must have gone out. For a while, her mind was fleeing from reality. Then she remembered the house in flames, the blazing fire which she still heard, but could no longer see. She reached out with her hands, desperately hoping to find the softness of her own bed, but her hands only grasped the air, and Senka realized that she was standing. Her nostrils filled again with the overpowering smell of things burning, and she coughed against the smoke. She wanted to turn away, but her legs fell out from under her. She collapsed to her knees, leaning with her hands onto the cold ground, the soil somehow fresh despite the sun and the fire, those warm blazes which she could no longer see. There was something so consoling in this ground beneath her fingers; the thin grass was pleasant to the touch, and Senka, for the first time in her life, simply wished to not exist.

She could not say how long she remained there, kneeling, not thinking about anything, when suddenly by her cheek she felt something soft and wet. Vidra! The dog had leaned his snout against her cheek, licking her, as if he wanted to say that he was still there, and that he was sorry for everything. Her dog. The one thing that remained for her in this world… Senka let out a loud sob and wailed, allowing the horror of all that had happened to pour out in a stream of tears. She cried long and hard, quietly and desperately, stroking her dog's head, hugging him around the neck and running her hands down his back and coat, remembering the look of her companion, pulling her dog closer and feeling his soft fur underneath her fingers.

This is how Senka felt the hair of her dog raise, and the unmoving body, which she had been holding for how long she could not say, came to life. She felt the push of the dog's nose at her side and immediately understood: move! Without words, almost silently, Senka lifted and leaned herself against the back of her dog. Her tears were still flowing, but the sense of horror was back. Fear, which had been suppressed by desperation, was beginning to swallow her fully. Senka rose up, holding tightly onto Vidra's back, as she had done many times before. Now, however, for the first time, that back was her crutch, her strength and her vision. The dog moved forward, and Senka followed; unsteadily and carefully, as if she was just learning to walk. And she learned indeed, both of them learned – the dog began moving more quickly than she could manage, and then slowed down when she nearly fell, adjusting his pace to hers. They had done this before, but it had always been a game. This now was a race for survival, even if Senka was only vaguely aware of it.

One step, and then another. At first, slowly and cautiously, and then a bit faster. Senka trusted Vidra, and her youth allowed her to adapt quickly. The dog felt danger, this she knew. She placed all of her faith in her companion, for there was nothing else left to her, and let the dog's instincts guide them, hopefully towards some sort of safety. Step by step. Senka had no idea how far they had gone or for how long they had been moving; she remained focused only on the next step. She could not see that darkness was approaching since for her everything was now dark. Even so, she became slowly aware of the change that the dog sensed. A strong grip of bitter cold began to reach her. A coldness which she had never felt before – not the sharp chill of a fresh winter day spent running through the snow with Vidra. No, this coldness was terrible, deathly, indescribable. The closest thing she had felt to this was when, as a child, she had touched the face of her dead midwife, the woman who had taken care of her after her mother had died and told her almost all she knew about her mother, much more than her father ever had; but it was her father who fell upon her after that touch and struck her with his hand, in front of everyone present at the funeral. It was one of the rare occasions that he had used such force on her, and Senka realized and remembered that what she had done was taboo, a forbidden and socially unacceptable thing. But now, this time, it was not she who had reached out and touched the cold – this coldness had reached for her, and closed about her. Stunned and bewildered, Senka collapsed once again.

She did not know that they had already arrived at the foot of the forest, and could not have known that the thick shadows of the trees were her only protection against a fatal destiny. Fear compelled her to silence, to bend as closely as she could to the ground, reduced to the panicked desire to disappear before an unseen danger. Yet the danger was much more real than she could have imagined.

Strange sounds began to reach Senka. Something like sniffling and creaking together, terrible sounds that leapt out from the sea of incoming noises, like some immense icy wave approaching. These strange noises overwhelmed the sounds of the fire, eclipsed the songs of birds in the distance, of crickets and flies, of the wind, and any other of the natural sounds of the forest. And then, Senka was at once alone in the dark, in complete silence, save for the unnatural noises. She was encircled by the approaching terror. Perhaps for a moment she fell unconscious, or perhaps not; it was difficult to judge in the constant, humming-filled darkness. Under her right hand, she felt the raised hair of Vidra. Like two shipwrecked sailors, they pressed against one another and as close to the earth as possible, holding firm to the solid ground below them, as if that patch of earth on which they lay was the one island in an endlessly dark sea, the only refuge for life in a deadly, frigid storm.

The sounds came even closer, like waves whipping the shore. Then, they seemed to cease. Senka held her breath as long as she could, trying to be so still that she herself could not hear her own breathing, not knowing whether that horror which they had been hearing was close or away. And then the sounds began to move off and fade. Senka and Vidra lay helplessly for a long while after, remaining so until Senka began to feel the dog's hair, little by little, relax. Whatever the danger had been, it had, for now, passed.

After what was likely an hour, Senka again raised herself. She had no idea where to go, nor what to do; she could not think clearly about such things, nor about anything else, so she did the same thing that had already saved her once, even if she was not fully aware of it; she gripped onto her dog's back with one hand, the other grasping about around her, and let Vidra lead them where he would... Far from the danger that, as she felt, was not gone for good.

– Chapter 4 –
Encounter One

"Damn horse! This one will not hold out much longer, tomorrow I will have to stop off at some village and get a new one..."

The hefty horseman had not said this very clearly however, as he was not particularly inclined to conversation. Everything that came out of his mouth sounded more or less like "Haaa!" interspersed with slappings on the horse's rump in an attempt to get the animal back to a quick trot. And truly, for a while the horse stopped pulling like a worn-out nag, even showing a fraction of its supposed value. All the same, the rider could not help the feeling that he had overpaid for it, like all those before, and again, frowning, he sank into a gloomy silence…

Suddenly, the horse stood as if stuck. The rider was pulled back from his wandering thoughts, instinctively repeating the slapping movement of his hand. His thwack, even though a bit harder than those before, this time did not prompt the horse to move one bit. Instead, the animal reared weakly, raising itself somewhat upright and uttered a paltry neigh. The heavy figure on its back then moved with astonishing speed – without a moment's thought, the man was off the horse's back, and in the same instant as his feet hit the ground, he was already holding his formidable weapon at the ready in his right hand.

Slowly and quietly, as much as possible for someone his size, the man made several steps toward the thick bushes that overlay the forest, leaving behind him the grateful animal who had been desperately awaiting an opportunity to catch its breath. As this man came up close to bushes, he grabbed the edge of a branch and swiftly pulled it aside, snorting gruffly through his thick mustache.

The bush gave way under this sudden jerk, and a good part of the plant remained in the hands of the giant man, torn, while the tearing squall of leaves and branches was accompanied by a muted scream and a threatening growl. The man stood back for a moment, the mace in his hand ready to strike, when his completely tense frame at once visibly relaxed, and he, lightly dropping his weaponed hand, spoke out clearly for the first time in many days:

"Well, well, look here, o wonder of wonders... what have we found at the forest's edge?"

– Chapter 5 –

A Night by the Forest

"Come on then, lassie, tell me once again… Something came after you, but you don't know what?"

If Senka were able to see, she would not have missed, even with her inexperienced eyes, the mocking expression in the eyes of her questioner. The enormous man raised up his waterskin, and gulped from it an amount that only he could call a sip. Then he smoothed out the two long sides of his mustache before addressing Senka again: "Talk, poor lassie, talk! Come on, string me along once again!"

And Senka again repeated her story to this strange man. He would now and again let out a few muffled sounds, which most likely signified wonder, or interest, or perhaps just a simple sign of attentiveness. The squeaking sound of the man's large waterskin opening reached Senka's ear more and more often, and from it the stranger swallowed larger and larger gulps. Without giving much thought to it, Senka had at first assumed that he was simply thirsty after a long days' journey. Shortly after their encounter, when she had said that she was thirsty and would like some water, it surprised her to no small degree that the man replied: "What? Water?!" with a tone of derision in his voice, "Water is bothersome in the boot, let alone in the stomach! I do not have water, I do not… but I have wine! Do you want some?" When Senka rejected the offer without hesitation, the man seemed to think for a moment, and then in his strange euphonious manner of speaking, almost melodious despite the masculine rudeness of his voice, said that there were numerous streams in the region and he certainly planned to make camp along one of them. And with that, the man decisively stood up and in one easy movement lifted Senka onto the back of his horse. Senka had never felt lighter! She had the impression that she was lifted without a trace of effort, and her impression was not false – the strength of the man was incredible and her weight was not enough to cause even the slightest tightening in his muscles. After setting her on the saddle, he hung his large wineskin up on the horn of the saddle, letting it fall against the horse's right flank, while tying his weapon, whose look alone would surely have frightened Senka could she see it, to hang to the left, mumbling: "That should keep it in balance, not pulling here or there." He grabbed the horse by the reins, which he skillfully threw forward, turning them into a halter, and led his new party (a horse, a dog, and a blind girl) where he wanted. Just like the horse, the dog and Senka both accepted, without a word, this unknown man as their undisputed leader.

And so soon they found themselves sitting beside a small fire, just alongside a brook they could hear clearly babbling away, and Senka, no longer thirsty or tired, retold yet again what had happened to her. The man listened, leaning back against a thick tree, and sitting so, drinking and listening, his head would now and again fall forward, until he finally drifted off to sleep. Senka continued to speak awhile about how she and Vidra had lain unmoving for how long no one could say, revisiting that horror once more, until the heavy snoring sigh of the man interrupted her story, assuring her that he was indeed sound asleep. Then she finally fell silent, and the quiet of the night confirmed her doubts. Wrapping herself up as best as she could, Senka lay down on the ground and fell asleep, tight against her dog once again. Her tormented spirit found, with unexpected ease, at least a moment's peace in the face of tomorrow's trials.

– Chapter 6 –

Who is Žarko

"What to do with you, lassie? To lead you onwards would not do, but to leave you here is worse!" These words the strange man spoke more for himself than anything else, the longest string of words Senka had heard him say during the whole morning. She felt desperately like crying, like pleading for herself, for help, to throw herself into his arms... but she remained silent. They were eating the leftovers from the night before, some kind of tasty meat which the rider had carried along with him under his saddle, very likely the last bits of some wild game which the man had himself hunted.

After a few more minutes during which Senka ate in silence, the mustached man announced his decision: "For now you will stay with Žarko, until we find you a home." This time Senka could not stand to wait and immediately asked: "And who is Žarko?" This triggered an eruption of laughter from the man. This gargantuan laugh, which hardly resembled a laugh as one would normally think of it, went on and on, and it seemed like the man was barely able to catch his breath as he replied: "Who is... har-har-har... who is... why, it's *me*, you poor thing! I am Žarko, who else would it be?!" And so Senka, just then, finally learned the name of her odd companion, even though she had already (more than once!) recounted the details of her recent calamities for him, as well as the brief story of her life.

And off they headed, the man announcing resolutely that it was time to depart. Senka did not know where to, but she also did not care; in the company of this man she felt more secure than she had ever felt in her short life, not really knowing why. As opposed to the evening before, when he had placed her on the back of his horse as he led, her companion now showed far less gentleness – Senka went on foot behind the horse, holding on to its tail with one hand, and onto Vidra with her other. The stranger kept the horse to a light pace, and this with no trouble whatsoever; any observer would certainly see that the animal was already overburdened by the size and weight of such a rider alone, and the walk was likely what the horse would choose anyhow.

Senka would have been, if she were to think about it, surprised by the speed at which she adapted to life without sight. Her eyes were now Vidra, and her step was perfectly aligned with the rhythm of the hoofs of the horse whose tail she held onto. And she felt safe. She did not stumble, but already stepped firmly, sure that this strange rider was already choosing a way for her. Everything was happening so fast that she did not have time to acknowledge, let alone grieve for, what she had lost, and her young spirit had become almost immediately accustomed to this unexpected adventure that now made up her life. She did not know what tomorrow held, or even what to expect in an hour or two, but that was exactly what she had longed for in the unmeasured days of her carefree, but also monotonous and fairly lonely childhood. She had dreamed of far away places, and now she was on her way to them. She has lost everything, but all that she had lost had already begun to look more and more like a far-off dream, like the sad story of some other person. Having lost her eyesight, security, and the chores of ordinary life, forced by cruel fate to rely on previously neglected senses and on chance encounters with strangers,

Senka was reborn as a new person. She was open to the world around her, for there was nothing left to grab onto in fear of what might come. Deprived of every support, this girl of twelve was forced to fly like a leaf swept off a tree. And now she flew, aware of every step, every word, every sound, every moment. Senka was alive.

"There, a village near the road. I will fill my wineskin there… and buy a decent horse, because this old nag is at her end." Senka realized that she was enjoying all of these rare proclamations of her protector, for that is how she had thought of him since the first moment they met. His statements were guideposts, dictating the direction of her current life. And this last one seemed prophetic: as soon as the rider spoke these words, the horse just collapsed underneath him! "There! See, I said so and I did not lie!" shouted the man with a dose of droll complacency, and then, without wasting another moment, he took upon himself all the things that the horse had been carrying with difficulty. After he slung his heavy weapon about his belt on the left side, he went onwards, allowing Senka to grab on to the muscle of his right arm. He even merrily whistled something almost like a tune. The village was close by, and he was pleased that the remaining walk would not last long.

And so they went forward, leaving the dead horse (or dead-tired, Senka was not sure) behind them. They went along on the only sort of road that Senka had ever known; not the one paved with cobblestones, like those supposedly known to larger places and towns, which her father had once spoken of (this sudden thought of her father elicited a brief wave of sadness), but rather an ordinary path of stamped earth, occasionally rutted and collapsed, just wide enough for the passage of a horse and wagon – in the rare event that two horse carts might meet going in opposite directions, one of them would have to stop and turn off of the path so that the other could pass.

After a short while, the familiar sounds of a settled area began to reach Senka. The road led right through the village, even widening a measure, unlike those "real" roads which her father had spoken of, which would skirt about the edges of towns rather then lead into them. She could not grasp that only by hearing, but this village was not much bigger than the only other settlement she had seen before, and also looked more or less the same. A bit more than a hundred souls, dwelling in twenty or so houses. In the middle of the village stood a small tavern where one could get a drink, a meal, or a place to sleep for the rare traveler passing through, and just across the road was the one and only store in which one could find anything and everything: from foodstuffs and small items, to weapons and tools, and even horses, which were kept in a stable behind the shop. The road became flatter, and Senka no longer needed to lean so heavily on Žarko's arm. For a moment she thought to completely let go; she wasn't sure how the villagers would look at the sight of a blind girl holding onto the forearm of a large man instead of a stick, or whether Žarko might feel uncomfortable because of it. But her companion walked on in at an unbroken pace, with that same natural confidence which Senka had already learned to appreciate, so she simply relaxed and continued to curiously listen and take in the world around her.

– Chapter 7 –
Encounter Two

They were somewhere near the tavern, which Žarko first headed for, when they heard the mob. Senka realized that something was happening from the sound of rough shouts and the unusual uproar, and immediately felt uneasy, while Žarko stood calmly in the middle of the street. He was interestedly following the goings on, just as his young companion once upon a time would raise a glance at any bird singing in the forest.

While they stood so in the open, Senka began to grow more fearful as she began to pick apart some of the shouted words rising above the clamor.

"Žarko, what is happening?"

"They have caught some thief, so they are going to chop off his hand." Senka's horror grew even greater at the calm and dispassionate way in which he said this.

"They cannot do that!" she murmured in disbelief.

"O, but they can… the law says so," answered Žarko.

Then the piercing shrieks of the captured man reached Senka, as he pleaded with all of his voice: "Please do not, people…. Please, for god's sake, do not… Please not my hand; I am already crippled in the leg!"

What exactly happened in Senka's heart at that moment, what broke within her, is hard to say. But she managed to overcome the stifling fear and the sudden shock at the terrible thing this angry mob was preparing to do in the name of justice. Something in her made a snap decision that stood in complete contrast to her actual abilities, and she screamed out: "Žarko, we cannot let them do it!"

"What are you talking about, you poor thing, do not be a fool!" Žarko hushed her up harshly. But if she could see his gaze, she would have known that he had spoken to her more moderately than he wanted to. This was not a man prone to delicacy.

"Please, Žarko! Please, please, please! You are so big and powerful, a true hero! You must not let this poor man suffer in front of you! He stole, did a bad thing, but they want to cut off his hand! They want to take away his hand, Žarko, and maybe he just stole a mere hen so he could eat! You heard that he is crippled, maybe he cannot work for his own food! Like me, Žarko – what would I do if I had not met you? How would I find something to eat? Žarko, you cannot let them do it! Please, Žarko, I plead before the God of the heavens, please, please, please!" Senka was on the verge of hysteria, tears running out of her eyes. There was no explanation for her behavior; she simply felt that her new world, whose foundation had just been built, would collapse into dust if she would allow this barbarity to happen in front of her protector's eyes. For she had already blindly built a vision of her crude companion against the gods – as ill-tempered but righteous, as mighty yet merciful. And she could not allow herself to see him as cold-hearted; he could not be someone who would indifferently watch the mob abuse the weak.

Though he would never have admitted it to a living soul, not even to himself, Žarko was moved by the girl's pleas. This powerless, young soul begging so desperately on behalf of an unknown and even unseen person in spite of all the tragedies she alone had already faced, struck a chord in Žarko's heart. She had even reached out to the sleeping God of the heavens, not for herself, but for the fate of a stranger! He himself would never think to meddle in such a situation – the thief had stolen and had been caught, and the law commanded that he be punished. Žarko did not write the laws, and he also did not bother to think about whether they were just or not. He repeatedly violated them himself, killing those shielded by the law even though they deserved death, yet his head had always remained on his shoulders. The times in which they lived were shaped by people like him, a thing he felt unconsciously, though such thoughts were too subtle to ever be expressed in words. The law of might instead of the might of law was often the reality, the unwritten truth above the official laws of towns: for the laws to be enforced properly, a righteous force had to be behind them, and where such force was lacking, strength alone prevailed.

Žarko carefully scrutinized the bedlam in front of him. Twenty or so villagers, perhaps more, two holding the thief tightly by the hands, dragging him forward to the place where they intended to carry out his punishment, with others going out of their way to beat him, kick him, and spit on him. Some other men of the village were surely still out in the fields plowing or pasturing their cattle, while the remainder of the settlement was likely made up of women, children, and the elderly. He saw their heads peeking out from some of the houses, through windows, and all of them stared, following the furor unfolding; the capture of the thief had overshadowed even their arrival in the village, which would ordinarily have been a real spectacle for such a place. Only some of the men from the procession carried arms, if just some rough pitchforks or worn out hoes, and they used them to poke the thief crudely in the back; they were, obviously, peasants, and not warriors. Žarko had not actually regarded the thief at all – he was not interested in him in the least, even though he was close to deciding to help him and so change the course of that pathetic fate.

"You speak well, dear little sister… your words are pure, but what you spout is madness! Nevertheless, Žarko will do what you wish, as it is too heavy a day for bloodshed." And just like that, a momentous decision had been reached. For, such was he a giant among men – what others would think over for days and days, he decided in seconds, according to the whims of his mood. And once he decided, Žarko acted with all of his might. He nudged Senka towards the tavern door, across the street's pavement stones, rushing her out of the way while putting the empty wineskin into her hand, at the same time pulling out his mace with his other hand: "Come on, little sister… do not stand here, go get me my wine; say to them: 'Žarko ordered it.' Who knows what will happen after, and I need to fill up." While still speaking these words, he had already moved towards the mob. A few huge steps and he was close enough, so he halted in the middle of the dusty street, exclaiming:

"Hey, villagers, hear me out!" Žarko's booming voice rose above the noises and in a moment there was silence, the people all turning their heads towards him as if under command. Then the mighty man continued: "Tell me, who among you knows to read and write? Who of you has read the books of old?"

In the mob there was confusion as some of the men looked around at each other questioningly. Silence reigned. Then one voice shouted falteringly that there was no one literate in the village, before abruptly falling silent. Žarko stood there, upright, gazing at the crowd. Frowning grumpily as he was, this big man was a terrible sight to behold. His spectacular figure stood at least a head higher than anyone's in the village, and in broadness he was twice the man of the largest peasant. On his head the wolf cap, its upper jaw extending over his brows; on his chest the wolf pelt, a furry vest he wore inverted. In his hand the heavy mace, behind his back the battle spear, and in his belt the saber. The two huge sides of his mustache relaxed somewhat, as he continued looking at the peasants, saying nothing… Little by little the villagers grew uneasy, and nervous mutterings and muffled whisperings could be heard among the mob. Only then did Žarko speak again:

"With no one who reads or writes, how then can you know the law?" Silence. Nobody ventured a word, though nervousness seemed to be growing in the crowd, as if it could sense impending trouble in the air. Žarko again stood silently, regarding them for a time, and then spoke:

"Well, here is Žarko, standing alone in front of you all! And I tell you: I know both, to read and write. The one who thinks he knows the old books better, has to cut off Žarko's hand first, and only then the thief's!" After saying this, the giant of a man suggestively moved that heavy mace in his right hand, letting it swing gently back and forth. The mumbling in the mob stopped fully, and silence hung, as if echoing in their ears. And it lasted. It lingered in the air like the people's fear – it was one thing to catch a hobbled thief, but quite another to confront a fierce warrior. No one risked a word, let alone rose up against Žarko. Žarko left them hanging for a while, staring at them grimly, one by one. And whoever he glared at, the other man's gaze would drop. Then he raised his voice once again:

"Look here, look here… no one knows the book of law better than the warrior Žarko? If that is how it is, I will take that thief as a slave. I will pay you fairly for the damage he has done; and I say: this is by the law. If someone disagrees with this, come forth now, complain to Žarko!" And, saying this, he scowled even more menacingly, which would have been thought unbelievable just a minute before.

Again one could hear whisperings from the crowd, more strongly even, but now no longer so agitated. The mob had calmed when faced with danger, the man from whom the thief had stolen shouted his consent from the safety of the crowd, while others used this opportunity to already begin slipping away. And so it was resolved; the two men holding the thief by the arms led him up to Žarko, somewhat hesitantly, their heads bowed and their eyes on the ground. They released him and then quickly turned back. The village street emptied, even the man to whom damages were to be paid went away, saying there was no need, that he would not want to take money from such a warrior. Then Žarko, watching the last few people scattering, addressed the thief: "With me, if you value your head." Then he turned, not looking at him again, and headed straight for the tavern. Senka had not, of course, filled the wine – like everyone else, she had been caught up in the excitement of the events, and had not moved from the entrance, listening, all the time holding the empty wineskin in her hand.

And while the whole village still lingered in a daze under the powerful impressions of what had just occurred, Žarko had already devoted himself to other things. He sent a scared barmaid to fill up his wineskin and fetch the innkeeper; when the man came out, visibly frightened, Žarko asked him to estimate how much was owed to the man from whom the thief had stolen, as he did not want to have a debt to anyone. He told Senka and his new drudge to wait in the tavern while he went across to buy a horse, enough bread, and one whole, uncooked lamb, skinned and well-salted, then threw all of that onto the horse and came back. He reentered the tavern and told the thief, for the first time looking him straight in the eye, grimly: "Now I will eat and drink with my sister until the time for heading out. And you, my servant, will wait in front… Watch the horse! When I come out, if you are not here, or my horse is not here, know there is no place nor hole under the heavens where you can crawl in to hide from me!"

– Chapter 8 –
A Thief Named Vuk

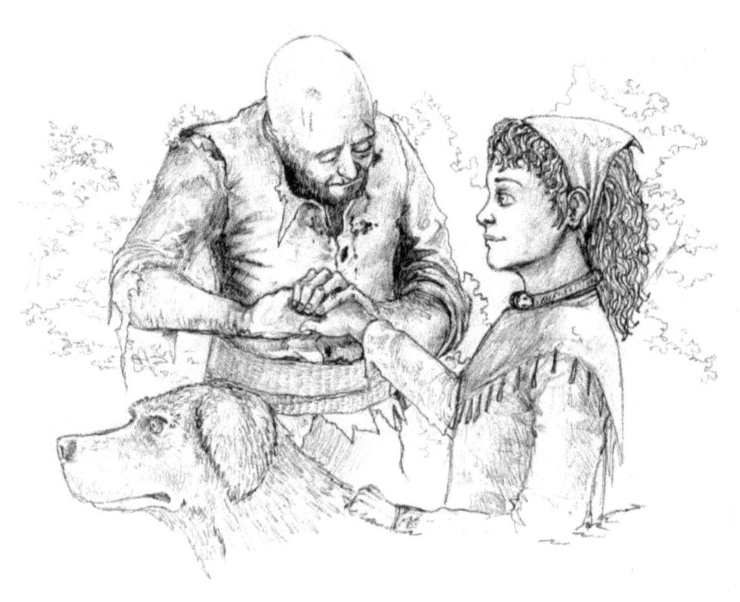

"Eh, my Žarko... who have you gathered around you? First a blind girl, now a cripple! Without a doubt, an impressive lot..." The big man went on, occasionally muttering to himself under his breath, allowing the horse that was carrying both him and food to wander off relatively far in front of his companions. Senka shivered at the thought of how upset Žarko would be if he also knew of her illness, which seemed to return at the worst moments, but she quickly dispelled such thoughts – she did not want, not even in the slightest, to be an even greater burden to her protector.

When the saved man figured that Žarko could no longer hear him, he spoke for the first time, addressing Senka, who was walking unsteadily alongside him. "Thank you," he said, "as I assume that you have played a large role in my unexpected salvation. I am sure that a warrior such as Žarko would not even look back once at a fellow such as me – it is you that I have to thank for still having two of these." With that, he extended both his hands and folded them about Senka's – her free hand, the other was holding constantly onto Vidra's back – saying: "My name is Vuk, and I am eternally in your debt."

Senka opened up unusually easily to this strange man. Thief! Her father had spoken about such persons with disgust, yet something in the tone of his voice assured Senka that every word this man uttered was true. He was not looking for explanations, but Senka offered them anyway. He had not asked, but Senka told him the whole story of the strange events that had fundamentally changed the course of her life, and which had led her to hang on the back of the rough warrior who was now her guide and guardian. After listening to her story all the way up to her first encounter with Žarko, the man who limped audibly next to her left side suddenly sighed strangely, and Senka left off her tale in mid-sentence. Taking this as an invitation, the silent Vuk spoke.

"And up till now you have not yet asked yourself who he is? Who is this man who saved you, and then me?"

Senka was confused by the question. "Well, he is Žarko. Or at least that is what he said his name is..."

Vuk spoke on in a completely serious voice, so Senka remained unconscious of his smile: "And truly, that is how he is called. I know, because I have heard stories about him in all the villages and cities through which I have passed, from the shores of Ohrid to the foothills of Mount Miroč. That is Žarko. Everyone knows of him. The greatest warrior-hero, the bravest, the strongest, and, though fiery and dangerous, always just. And yet all the stories of him seem to pass around him. Did you notice how in that village he did not know anybody, even though everybody seemed to have known him? Perhaps... well, I would not be surprised if they had seen him before, for that kind of fear in an entire mob cannot be caused by just one man, even one as large and strong as he, no matter who he says he is and how imposing he appears..."

Vuk fell silent. They continued far behind the big man on the horse for several minutes, and Senka realized that the limping man was thinking over whether to continue speaking further. Though now quite curious, the girl remained quiet, letting him reach his decision. Finally, Vuk abruptly continued on with his story, just as suddenly as he had fallen silent.

"In a small town, in a tavern, quite some time ago, after a great deal of wine and even more beer, I heard a strange story. Now, like any other story, it may be true, and it may be not. I found it hard to believe it that day, but now I am not so sure…" Vuk paused as if to take a breath, then continued: "The story speaks of a great warrior-hero, the son of a god, who was named Žarko. It is said that this hero was the son of Perun the Thunderer himself, while his mother was a mortal woman. And so they say there was nothing other for that child but to become the greatest of all warriors…" A short silence arose and lingered for some moments, and Senka felt that Vuk was cautiously observing her reactions to his story, perhaps weighing whether his words seemed too unbelievable. At last though, as if having pushed through some troublesome barrier, he broke the suspenseful silence and the rest of his narration proceeded without a single pause.

"Yet, only when that child had indeed grown into a warrior like no other, did this story become truly interesting. If I was lied to, then I am lying to you now as well, but it is said that it was the time when the gods were clashing over the division of our world. More precisely, over who will be given charge of the lands through which we are now passing. And as you might imagine, agreements are not reached easily among the gods, those gods you know well and those you may not know of at all. Conflict seemed inevitable, and who knows what would come of it, had not the gods, in their final attempt to resolve the division of the world, sought the opinion of someone outside of their circle. And, well, who could offer such an opinion better than the greatest warrior of our world, the son of the god of justice and lightning, and thus comparable to those beyond compare. The most powerful among the gods assented to this resolution – even though he could have taken what he wanted by force – for the sake of avoiding conflict, believing that his own earthly son would surely rule in his father's favor. And so messengers were sent out for him, powerful horsemen who could trample over all in their path, but who bowed before such a warrior. They told him that the gods were quarreling, and that he had been called on to say who should rule over the lands. The gods believed, at least as the narrator told, that: '*Žarko will decide this justly, for Žarko fears no one.*' And not only did he not fear, but his mother had advised him before her passing: '*Žarko, my son, my one and only, do not speak wrongly, neither for your father's behoof, nor in the behoof of uncles, but speak with the true righteousness of the god of justice! Truth is stronger than any sword, it will be your sharpest weapon.*' And so the hero went to pronounce judgement on those who judge…

"Of course, for the story to be interesting, the righteous division of the world that would be proclaimed would in the end please the god of justice the least! For who can judge the bringer of justice itself?" Vuk here laughed a bit to himself and continued on in a quiet voice, all the time taking care that the horseman in front of them could not make out what they were speaking of. "You see, Žarko proceeded to scold the gods well, each god in his turn, sparing not even his own father. He told them that they had become lost in their conflicts, that they scrambled for lands that were not theirs. He told them that this was the kingdom of Dajbog, made for him by Svarog, the Creator, out of the darkness of his first dream, for his first son only. He told them, he told the descendant gods: '*From the father it dawned upon the son, the first son of God almighty!*' When Perun the Thunderer, the mightiest god of this world, heard this verdict, one which he never could have expected, he grew red with rage. He jumped at his son, striking him with thunderbolts, and he, even the great warrior-hero that he was, ran: he ran away as fast as his legs could carry him. For he did not think it right to fight against his own parent, a fight he would also be sure to lose. And it was then that he would have died, as the story goes, had not his angel interfered: like a cloud of light, the angel descended in front of the enraged god only to be struck by a thuderbolt that would surely have killed the god's son. This guardian had sacrificed his immortal life for the life of Žarko, and so was he left without his angel, unlike you, me, and all other people of this world, and therefore there is no one left to take him to that other world when his time comes... And so our hero escaped, yet the consequences of this judgement he voiced unto the gods, he carries with him to this day. Perun cursed him while Dajbog blessed him, and both of these legacies have made him what he is today."

Vuk now dropped his voice almost to a whisper, more and more careful that a stray word not accidentally reaches Žarko's ears. "I think that I memorized word for word all that I heard that night in the tavern. It is said that

Perun proclaimed the following: '*Žarko, my son – may God strike you dead! You shall know no grave nor kin, bereaved of throne and origin! You will wander without end! May your soul never ascend before to the conqueror you bend!*' Perun cursed him, but with this came also Dajbog's blessing: '*My brave Žarko, God still smiles upon you! You are lit by heaven's light, you will strike forever right! There shall be no greater hero! Your name shall be ever spoken while there shine the Sun and Moon!*' And much of what was proclaimed has come to be, though some of it may yet..."

And here again Vuk sank into silence, broken by the occasional sound of his limping feet pulling across their path. Senka remained alone for a while in the grasp of the story, taking time to gather her impressions. "And you think that..." she finally uttered. "I do not think anything!" Vuk interrupted. "It is just a tavern story."

After another pause, however, he could not refrain from speaking his mind. "And yet, here we are, followers of perhaps the greatest of heroes, whose name is known by all. A warrior who wanders from village to village, from town to town, and knows nobody anywhere, though everyone knows him. A hero whose accomplishments are so much greater than could be accomplished in a single human life. A warrior who men look upon in fear, and women with adoration. But who, in spite of everything, remains alone, just like you and I..." And Vuk drew in a long breath, during which it seemed that he was preparing the great conclusion of his story: "I do not think nor claim anything... yet, there you have it, if anywhere in this world exists one man who can die only by the will of the Creator, God of all gods, I would be willing to bet my freshly-spared hand that he is riding on the horse ahead of us."

– Chapter 9 –
Infernal Pack

The small group which had headed out from the village and upon their journey in the late afternoon, as the sun began to drop, travelled on for as long as Žarko could make out the path in front of them. After a peaceful night, another calm day of travelling followed, with a long afternoon break. Senka had the impression that Žarko had no particular goal in mind, but neither she, and even less so Vuk, dared to inquire about this. They left all decisions to the hulking man on the horse, and were pleased to stay back and disturb him as little as possible, as he had been in a sullen mood ever since they had left the village.

Another evening was approaching, which Senka could sense from the pleasant shift in the air and the tiredness in her legs. The third evening of her new life! And an evening during which she would finally become aware that, through no will of her own, she had set into motion strange forces which, from then on, would shape not only her fate, but also the fates of her companions… While the sun was slipping slowly into the horizon, a harbinger was approaching. It started simply – Žarko had suddenly stopped his new horse, cursing at him for being disturbed.

"What is with this nag now? As if it is scared of something…" he grunted, more to himself than to Senka or Vuk. Then he turned around and looked. It is difficult to say what followed: did Žarko, because of what he had seen, first cast out a voice that signified the danger, or did Senka unconsciously lean towards the ground, crouching with a muffled scream, because of what she suddenly felt and immediately recognized. Even the ever-quiet Vuk let out a long and prolonged "uhoooo…" And at that moment, they all began to hear what were at first barely audible sounds, but which quickly became a sea of noise that steadily approached. Together with these strange noises, as if to intensify their unpleasantness, a bone-chilling cold began to prickle them, biting at their goosebumped skin; still only in hints, like small waves rolling over the shore, yet nevertheless telling of the deep dark sea behind. And again it seemed well for Senka that she was not able to see what Žarko and Vuk were staring upon: the darkness approaching.

Vuk felt fear; a fear greater than any he had known before, beyond even that which he had experienced the last day in the village when they were about to cut off his hand. Yet despite his entire body telling him to flee, he stared, as if bewitched, at the coming gloom. At first glance, it looked like a dark cloud rolling across the ground or a black apparition crawling over the earth. Whether because of the increasing closeness of the horror or their spellbound gaping at it, it seemed that the dark mass started forming parts of lesser or greater darkness, small figures who were growing in size. And very quickly in this multitude of shapes it was possible to clearly discern the dark horseman at the forefront – robed all in black, riding on a coal-black horse that was galloping towards them, standing out as the sharp spearhead pulling the whole wave and spurring it forward. To the left and right of him, forming the shape of an arrow whose striking point was the rider, dark animals sprinted. "Wolves," gasped the hobbled thief. But these were not the type of wolves from which his name had been drawn. There was nothing natural in these dismal shapes that approached them with blinding speed. All of them were entirely black, but for their fiery eyes, which seemed to shine out a piercing red, or so it seemed against the dark surge around them; and they were much larger than any ordinary wolf was meant to be, as could be seen by the size of those running closest to the horse. Above this hellish pack and the rider at the forefront, flurried what made the scene beyond ghastly – a cloud of dark, endlessly bustling bodies and wings, a swarm of creatures that, through their almost infinite number, produced the great din which had first reached the ears of our forlorn threesome. "Du... dusk imps," stammered a horrified Vuk. And he was right – these were ghoulish things he occasionally heard mentioned in frightful stories, little human-like things with wings like bats. Yet they could never be mistaken for real bats: the small fire they sporadically spit from their mouths made it look as if, advancing toward them, was a night sky pulsing with a swarm of disturbed stars that occasionally burned and flashed quickly, revealing for a moment the terrifying form behind each one. From the stories that Vuk heard, but until now never believed in, he knew that such creatures could only be met in the dead of night; yet in spite of this, they were flying toward them while the sun was still hovering just at the horizon, furiously flapping their wings in an unnaturally tight grouping, as if to blot out any speck of light from ever reaching the ground. "Some witchcraft for sure..." murmured Žarko. His thoughts, however, were different; although he also carefully observed the grim ensemble approaching, perhaps frightened just as Senka and Vuk were, he looked at it all through the eyes of an experienced warrior; he was concerned not with what it was, but already with how to deal with it.

"I do not know if this is something I can combat, but you must run away – now! Hide and wait for me, for I mean to return!" He exclaimed this with a clear and firm voice, before forcing his struggling horse straight at the horror that was approaching.

It was not necessary for him to order them more than once to run. "This way!" shouted Vuk, and Senka pulled Vidra in the direction of his voice, then let her dog lead her, trusting once again in the animal's instincts. "Easy, Vidra!" she had to exclaim several times, as the dog's nerves drove him forward in haste and Senka followed him with difficulty, stumbling and falling to the ground frequently. "Just a bit further, into the woods!" she heard Vuk shouting from far ahead. Then, quite unexpectedly, in the middle of this rush, she heard a clear whisper, as if someone's mouth were pressed right onto her ear; she twitched, fearfully jumping away, but the voice continued to hiss: "Essscape… hide… Esssscape… hide!" And Senka continued running, holding tightly to Vidra.

"Sssstop… here... Ssstop… here!" the voice changed its command. Senka obeyed without thinking, throwing herself to the ground. She was already quite winded, though they had not been running for long. The dog dropped down at her side; they were hidden in the dark of the thick woods, well beyond the vulnerable edge of the forest. From searching eyes, they where shielded not only by the tree branches above, but also by the dense forest shrubs growing all around; were Senka able to see, she would have wondered how on earth had they managed to get through such a wall of bushes, and that without a single scratch. But she could not, just as she could not see Vuk. And Vuk was also a sight to behold: a cripple, who until now had barely been managing to pull his lame leg along the way, suddenly had taken off as if transformed into a hurried, frightened animal. He moved through the forest on all fours, now using his hands to rush more skillfully than his legs had served him earlier. He was bouncing around swiftly like a dog with a broken leg. Occasionally he would look back, trying to catch a glance of Senka. When he no longer saw her, he shouted her name out again, and, upon hearing a muffled response telling him that she was also hidden, stopped for a moment; then he scrambled immediately up to the top branches of a tree in a flash, displaying astonishing agility. Through the crowning branches of the trees he could follow what has happening back on the path they had been walking. Senka, despite all of Vuk's earlier stories, had never asked herself how such a crippled man could have travelled so widely across the world, nor how someone barely mobile could ever have managed to be a thief; and she had just missed a clear answer to her unspoken questions.

In the meantime, Žarko had drawn so close to the black cloud that his horse simply dug his hoofs in the ground, refusing to go a single step further, despite Žarko's attempt to spur it on with loud curses and slaps at its flanks. As the horse reared and stomped under the pressure of its determined rider, the advancing black cloud suddenly came to a halt – without any audible command, or perhaps one that was lost in the tremendous tumult of wingbeats and cries coming from the grotesque imps above. But a command had clearly been given: as one, simultaneously, the wolfish pack and the horseman at its helm paused, while a smothering of imps stopped to float in place, continuing to shade them. Then, after a slight pause, perhaps in hesitation, the rider separated himself from the dark mass and advanced forward. One horde of the imps also separated from their swarm, fluttering above the dark horseman like a miniature cloud; he was completely enshrouded in their shadows, making him seem even larger than he truly was, while at the same time obscuring clear sight of him despite the light of dusk still lingering. Žarko was hit by the full strength of that unearthly dread and cold which Senka had spoken of, and for a passing moment he too felt the desire to turn around and flee in the other direction. But even if he were to do so, he was unsure of what response he would get from his steed; the animal's snout was now covered in foam which gushed from its mouth, and was an immovable object, dug so deep into the dirt that it seemed rooted there. So there was no better choice for him – despite the horrible chill – but to wait there for the approaching darkness. Besides, he had an odd urge to see what this strange black rider looked like up close. If nothing else, the wolves had been mustered some way behind, and perhaps he could manage to battle and overthrow the horseman alone, before they could rush to his aid. As for the winged things flying everywhere above, Žarko would rather not give them a thought. Instead, with a slow motion he pulled forth his big mace from its straps, taking it in his right hand, shifting the jagged head over his shoulder softly and effortlessly, showing disdain along with menace, whilst all the while maintaining a rigid grip on the bridle ropes of the horse with his left hand, in case the animal were to go wild again. Let the darkness come to them.

The horseman and the winged cloud above halted just a few horselengths away from Žarko; he thought he could reach him with a few quick, deliberate jumps, if only his fool horse would obey him. Now the two riders surveyed one another, cautiously and inquisitively. Žarko knew full well the kind of impression he made on people when he scowled; he imagined that those people felt quite similar to how he was feeling at this moment. The horseman confronting him was downright frightful. Through the murkiness that accompanied him and the shadows that concealed him, he saw a heavy black piece of armor that covered his chest, and underneath that armor, a sheath of thick chain-link ringmail draped across his body like a shirt, dropping to his thighs; in his cloaked belt was a saber of enormous proportions, even by Žarko's measure, yet the horseman did not even rest his hand on its hilt, let alone have it pulled out. He was attired entirely in black, so uniformly dark that it was hard to discern any gaps between the armor, his sheath, and his legs. Žarko was barely able to observe that the rider wore full black gauntlets extending down his arm to his fingertips, and long black boots up to his knees – the only thing unblackened was his livid white face, bordered by his raven black hair draping down to his shoulders. This whole appearance elicited a strange impression – one that was sinister, yet at the same time lordly and almost beautiful. Whatever aberrant sort of beauty this was, it was tainted by the glow of his blood-stained eyes and red-blotched cheeks, and the deception in his posture and performance seemed obvious and purposeful, as if staged in a play just for Žarko's eyes to see.

But in examining him more closely, Žarko began to pick out details that seriously marred the original impression given off by the black rider: his black hair hung down in dirty whips, and his clothes at the folds were ragged, old, and worn. "This hair was not braided by handmaidens, these garments not washed by any servants," thought Žarko. And this thought gave him a fragment of sudden pleasure, inducing even a momentary smile. As if in answer to this smile, the rider in black tugged hard at the reins of his horse, which whinnied out a terrible screech. This momentarily undid Žarko's whiskered smile, prompting him to speak quickly and loudly.

"Hail to you, unknown knight! What good quest has brought you here, if god knowest?"

Then the horseman responded; to Žarko's great relief, since he was uncertain as to whether this spectre would speak at all. The voice was dry and crude, as if he spoke with effort; at the same time threatening and scratchy like a muffled growl, yet somehow entirely articulate, so that Žarko could clearly make out every spoken word:

"Know this, man, who recognize me not: a king-warrior I once was, but for long now, much more than that! And I know not what god you serve, but it surely is not mine… No, who are *you*, you crazed nomad rambler? Rare are men who dare to stand in my path, you should bow before me!"

Now Žarko felt emboldened, for this was his ground; he had been through such exchanges countless times. "Hear, warrior, in front of you stands Žarko: my path goes wherever I go, and I bow to no one! I am neither here for you, nor do I step down before thee."

The rider now seemed to smile himself: "So you are that Perunović Žarko…" His scowl was a parody of joy, horrific like the grinning of some rabid beast.

Žarko spoke again:

"And you seem to know me, stranger. But… I know not why you mention Perun, when I serve not him, nor any other god: honor to them all, but Žarko serves no one!"

The terrible smirk on the face of the horseman grew wider: "I know you well, you mad Žarko, at least from some stories. Who has not heard of Žarko the hero? But heed this, hero: it would be wise for you to get out of my way. I will not bother to scuffle with you, since I have nothing with you."

"You argue well, king-warrior, but you make do poorly! Tell me with whom you have something, and let us see where that leads." With these words, the smile vanished from the rider's face, yet Žarko almost enjoyed the scowl that replaced it, even if it was equally horrific when the black figure spoke again.

"Listen, Žarko: do not play the fool! I do no explaining, save to whom I serve now. And even then, only when I choose to, because I, too, bow or kneel to no one! But fine, if you wish to know, I will tell you this: I have an unresolved matter with that lass who fled me. Let me have her, so we may part on good terms."

At these words, the man with the mace frowned, unintendedly and openly. "Listen, stranger... as it happens, that little one is my sister in fate, made so by the will of the God of gods, the God of the heavens. As much as I might wish to, leave her to you I cannot, for that would be a great sin. And I would not let her go even if I had not become brother to her fate. Therefore, it is better that you just turn your great horse around, so that we can part peacefully!"

Then, there was silence. The horseman glared at Žarko, inquisitively, while Žarko gazed back at the rider defiantly. And then the black-tressed man laughed with his whole voice, a laugh as sharp as a knife's blade, raw and cruel. And short. After ridding himself of this hollow pretense of mirth as suddenly as it had begun, the rider spoke:

"Very well, Žarko, if that is how you want it to be, I

will allow it. Why clash here where there is no victory? My sabre might not be meant for your head… But think again, and think quickly, for in the dead of night my pack will set out in hunt. We will hunt for what is ours, and kill everything in the way. Kill, wound, or simply trample, it matters not. Beware, Žarko, that your path does not lead you across mine again!"

And after saying this, the horseman spurred and raised his horse, turned, and rode off, away from Žarko, followed by the high screams and wing flaps of the creatures above his invisible crown, not looking back even a single time. It was clear that he was not fearful of Žarko, and that made it even less clear as to why he would at all accept to withdraw. But while a biting chill still lingered, whether from the unnatural cold or the unmistakable threat which the stranger's final words held, Žarko finally allowed his limbs and body to relax somewhat. For the time being, they had pulled through. Yet it was now high time to ride off, and, reviving and turning his horse with a sudden twitch of reins, the large man spurred it into a full gallop, riding back to the spot where he had left his companions. Night was approaching. Long, perilous night.

– Chapter 10 –
Night Hunt

"You say, lass, that you know not why some are after you?"

The question was asked in a clearly doubting tone – and even someone as young as Senka, unsophisticated in conversation, could make out the clear disbelief expressed in this short sentence. They were now scrambling through the woods, as quickly as was possible. After coming together once again, Žarko told them that they must stray off the path. The forest would offer some semblance of shelter from the watchful eyes of their followers, even those above. This time the burly man was displaying a bit more sympathy, or rather the situation simply demanded it: either way, Senka and Vuk were now seated on the horse, while Žarko led it by the halter at a hasty step, quickly and decisively choosing a way through the forest dark. But if he had by any chance seen the rapidity with which the crippled man had moved just shortly before, on all fours, as he and the girl ran away, or the agility with which he had climbed up the tree and came down when he heard the gathering shouts, it would have made it immediately apparent as to how this supposed thief might have succeeded in such a vocation, and then they would probably have switched places on the horse. As they hastened, the dim light of the full moon would occasionally break through the branches above, signifying that the dangerous night had long ago already begun – thus far, however, there had been no sign of their pursuants. Yet the question of their whereabouts was far from the only one on Žarko's mind – his surly curiosity was far from abated. Beyond the still lingering question of why she was being followed was the essential mystery of *what* exactly it was that was after them…

"I do not know, Žarko. Truly, I do not." Senka was still frightened, along with bewildered by the tone of the question, so she was answering on the verge of tears.

"Really, sister? You have not, mistakenly or purposefully, concealed something?"

Žarko's questioning was now becoming too forceful for the girl. He never was a lover of mysteries, and here he was running from one, a completely terrifying one at that, and still unknowing of the reason. This was surely making him anything but pleasant to his companions. Senka again answered that she did not know who or what was following them, nor why. She was no longer able to withhold tears from slipping down her blind eyes – she felt as if she was losing the barely gained trust of her protector. From the tremble in her voice, Žarko made out that she had started crying, and softened his voice somewhat.

"Sis, come now... do not cry. But I must know from what are we running away – our heads depend on it. If I know what we are up against, then perhaps I can beat it. This is why I am asking: are you sure you have told me everything?"

For who knows which time, Senka again responded that she knew not a thing about their assailants. And Žarko fell back into a deep, unsettled silence, seemingly focused only on choosing their path, for he was no longer sure what to think or how to behave. As opposed to Vuk, he remained doubtful. While Vuk had fully accepted Senka's life story, like many other stories which he had listened to patiently and attentively over his years and journeys, Žarko saw it all as the fantasized tale of a poor orphaned girl: the sudden fire, the striking cold, the manner in which she had become blind... sure, he had been entertained by her minutely decorated story, even pressing her to tell it again and again and not finding any inconsistencies, but not for a moment had he believed any of it. Without much thought, he had come to the conclusion that the little girl had simply beautified her tragic story into a fantastic truth. Which was not so important, since for him in essence she remained exactly what she was: a blind orphan who asked for help. And he helped her. But now he was no longer certain… then, suddenly, he stopped the horse.

"The necklace. Let me see it, little sis."

For a moment, Senka did not understand, but then he was already standing beside her, trying to remove the necklace from her neck – the metal necklace which Senka called "the wrapped snake," and this was indeed its shape. He was not able to take it off, however, and the young girl let out a breath of relief, long held while he had fumbled with the smooth metal and then agitatedly turned away from her. That was the moment when Senka decided to say nothing of the snake's voice reappearing – she did not knew why Žarko would regard the wrapped snake as the source of their troubles, but she knew well that she wanted to dispel *any* kind of reason for her protector to forcefully remove the "necklace" that hung around her neck. Slightly astonished, she now suddenly realized she somehow trusted the snake that made her blind; disturbed, she envisioned telling them everything, fearing that some magic was influencing her will, but just then she felt a pleasant warming sensation around her neck, and the hint of a doubt which she had felt for a moment slipped from her mind.

They continued moving through the forest at a brisk pace, Žarko still in front leading the horse forward. Soon, from the noisy burbling of running water, Senka recognized that they had reached a wide stream – one that sounded very much alike to the one she had listened to so often back home. Their leader, without hesitation, stepped into the creek, pulling the horse along with him. Since the sound of the rushing water never left them, Senka realized that they were now actually marching onward in the stream itself. As if reading her mind, Vuk, who was sitting just behind her on the horse, leaned over and whispered into her ear: "We are following the brook downstream – this way the wolves will have a harder time picking up our tracks and scent. A very wise move, in my estimation, for we can perhaps fool them in such a way. Our fair leader is not only mighty, but also clever."

Time took on a different flow in their constant state of expectation. Senka could not say for how long they had been trekking through the water: minutes or hours, but she was alert constantly, all the while hoping not to hear the sound of those horrible wingbeats and cries and howling from behind her. After some time, she finally managed to single out a gentle splashing sound, quieter than the muffled steps of the horse's legs as it made its way through the water – Vidra had as well followed their example and was trotting in the stream just behind them. It made her proud, but all these sounds of water also made her suddenly realize that she was thirsty.

"Žarko, could we stop for a moment? So I can get down and drink some water?"

"No!" Vuk cried out. This was so sudden and unexpected that it startled Senka, while Žarko stopped and looked back at him. Vuk then explained more calmly: "The stories I have heard about the dusk imps, those ghastly little flying creatures, say they can poison an entire lake, so that anyone who drinks from it would fall dead from just one drop! This creek is flowing and so disperses the poison onwards, but we have no way of knowing whether the poison is in front of us or behind us, or whether we are walking through it at this very moment, if it is in the water at all. No, it is not safe to drink this water. It is not safe to drink any water we come across until we are certain that they are no longer following us; for now, we can rely only on the water we carry with us."

Žarko looked at him oddly: "What nonsense are you talking? Why carry when there is water at every step? And I have only wine. Perfectly good wine, mind you, and there is enough for all." At this offer, Senka mumbled that she was not so thirsty after all, and so they moved on down the stream, the hum of the water now tinged sinister.

Their march continued quietly, the party warily listening out for whether, above the mild murmur of the stream, that more disturbing buzz from above would be heard. And finally there it was – as if they knew it was bound to happen sooner or later. Žarko pulled at his horse to make a few brisk steps before coming to a stop under the cover of a large tree, still in the creek, with thick branches draping over them. There they stood in complete silence, as the perverse buzzing and shrieking came closer and closer. There was no need to say anything, as they all understood what loomed above them. The dreadful scouts were likely flying over the forest in every direction, looking for the girl. Senka held her breath, as if these flying things above could hear even her breathing. There they stood, motionless and waiting, as if petrified, even when the sounds of that infernal swarm had seemingly moved farther away. Only when the distant sounds were utterly drowned in the gentle humming of the stream did Žarko pull at his horse silently, nodding thoughtfully for them to continue. Judging by this recent arrival of the spying scouts, it must have been close to midnight, as the dead of night had been marked as the beginning of the hunt. They remained speechless, still pensive and anxious. Soon they would likely know whether they had succeeded in covering their tracks, though actual safety and survival were still far and away, with many long hours of night ahead.

– Chapter II –
Morlak

Only now did Senka begin to fathom what the "dead of night" truly meant. Midnight had arrived, and they all felt it. As if everything in the forest had fallen asleep or died: the breeze trailed off, the occasional night cries of birds ceased, even the owls stopped hooting, and even the stream's steady whisper seemed to hush, so that their wading through water suddenly sounded loud and heavy, as the silence wrapped around them like a shroud. And then, abruptly, the still of the witching hour was broken by a distant howl, a long, drawn out moan from the throat of a lone animal, stretching out and out and out until, finally, another wailing voice returned its call… and then another, and another, again and again, until these outcries of numerous throats had seemingly encircled the forest, pouring out into the night air. It seemed as if this choir of howls was coming from every direction. Luckily, still from a distance.

Žarko halted on the spot once again. Vuk thought that even the decisive warrior no longer knew where to lead them next. They appeared to be surrounded; in her head, Senka imagined a noose of demon wolves slowly tightening around them. Had they indeed fooled the wolves by covering their trail? Or had they simply fooled themselves beyond any chance of escape? Then the leader of the small fugitive party tugged again at the reins of his horse, leading them out of the stream.

Senka, of course, could not see where they were going; nor did Vuk at first grasp what was happening, until he observed something completely unexpected – there, in the middle of the forest, just a stone's throw from the edge of the creek, stood some small wooden shack! Žarko stepped out of the water and slowly led his horse towards this cabin, while trying to stay in the deeper shade of the tallest trees. The forest here seemed unnaturally bathed in the strong light of the full moon. As they approached the cottage, Vuk saw the outlines of another behind it, and then another, and yet another! Incredible – what was this, a village in the middle of the forest?! When they got closer, they could see that the huts were grouped about the edge of a small forest clearing, just beside which flowed the small stream they had just left. The moonlight now illuminated these cabins clearly. All of them but one were small, humble cottages, thrown together without a great amount of craft or skill, or perhaps just worn down by age, while at the center of the perfect circle that they formed stood a larger and more significant structure, close in size to the burned down house that Senka had once called home. Small forest trees were growing right next to the small huts, their branches protruding from the circle's outer edges and covering the huts in part. Only around the largest one in the middle, built just as low as all the others, was a small open area, just wide enough for few people to pass. From this circle, miraculously set apart from and yet in the thick of the woods, nothing could be heard to disturb the forest peace. There were no stables, no signs of livestock, poultry or horses, nor anything else characteristic of village life. There was nothing by which one might say that anyone lived there at all – the settlement might have been long deserted.

"What in the devil is this ghost town…" mumbled Žarko into his chest, quietly, eyeing the scene in front of him. They stood on the edge of the clearing, looking through a small gap between two of the cabins, and, as far as they could see to the left and right of themselves, there was not a single path leading through the woods to this abandoned place. It was as if some demon had snatched up a handful of huts from somewhere and planted them right here in the middle of the forest. Vuk shuddered from a sudden, unexpected chill and felt a desire to turn back to the stream from which they had just come, to move away from this place as soon as possible, but Žarko, for reasons unclear, stepped bravely forward. He cautiously led the horse through the narrow space, advancing towards the wooden hut at the center. Strange was this unlikely procession made up of a burly man leading a horse with a blind girl and lame thief, trailed by a silently walking dog. And thus the small party wandered into Morlak.

Nothing happened as they stepped slowly forward. There were no threatening signs that might signal an ambush as they went out onto the small open space in front of the central building. They found themselves near the entrance to the larger hut – only later would Vuk realize this was always the case, no matter which direction one entered the round village from – and Žarko led them straight towards the door. He seemed almost entranced, offering no explanations or indications of his actions, though perhaps he only wished to not break the odd, absolute silence of the place. Step by step, he approached the entrance, lit up by the light of the moon. They were just a few short steps away from the door, when the village awoke!

It happened so incredibly quickly, and yet at the same time completely naturally, that it seemed as if there was nothing unusual about it. The door in front of them opened without a sound, and at the door stood a figure lit up from the back by firelight coming from within. And where, just a moment before, there was a musty darkness lit only by moonlight and enshrouded in a deep silence, there was now the vibrant blaze of numerous hearths and the pleasantly muffled murmur of a living settlement. Vuk could not unriddle how it had happened – the hearths could not have begun glowing all at once, together and suddenly, yet he was sure that there had not been even a single fire lit as they moved through the small passage between the huts. Now, however, a little light was gleaming out from every single hut, glimmering beneath the doors or through a few small window panes.

The figure before them stood motionlessly, its face remaining in the darkness, but the light from behind clearly outlined a large figure – an imposing man, bearded, and almost as great in stature as Žarko. And he just stood there, staring fixedly at them. Vuk noticed uneasily that the doors of all the other huts he could see had opened, and before each one there was now someone standing. All these doors were facing the center of the circle and the larger dwelling in front of them. They were surrounded and lost, while all the eyes of the village were focused on the strangers. Then, slowly, the villagers began approaching. There was nothing threatening in their movement; the horse and the dog could sense this, and they showed no sign of uneasiness. And so the fugitives were suddenly surrounded by people who were looking at them curiously. The only one who did not approach was the man at the door of the largest building, but they were already within his reach; then, as if he had been waiting for the others to gather round, he spoke out. He had a deep masculine voice, rough but at the same time inexpressibly pleasant: "I welcome you, travellers, to Morlak! Rare is the opportunity to host passers-by in our little village. Dismount and come inside, for it is time to feast!"

As could be expected, Žarko was the first to bounce back into senses, while Senka and Vuk were still completely confused: "Dear host, thank you, may fortune favor you! We would gladly eat and drink, but now is not the time; trouble is upon us, we are being hounded…"

"Put your worries aside, hero," the large man at the door interrupted Žarko. "Here time flows differently than the stream you stepped out of. So come on in, dear guests, make yourself comfortable, and let us celebrate. There is time." And with these words, the man turned around and vanished back through the doorway from which he had appeared.

– Chapter 12 –
Feast

They were sitting in the central cabin, which Vuk perceived as some kind of unusual tavern. Everybody was seated on low, rough-hewn tree trunks, surrounding a large, round, wooden table, the only one in the whole large-roomed hut: Žarko, Senka and Vuk, along with another ten or so men. There were apparently no women in the village, or at least at the table. And the men were all hardened and strong, as if all coming from the same mold. They were dressed humbly, in fur vests similar to Žarko's own, which revealed their sturdy muscles and broad chests. Except for some rough pants, also made from animal skins, which barely reached below their knees, they wore nothing else. No one carried any kind of weapon, and every single one of them was barefoot.

On the table in front of them were water, wine, and beer in simple pitchers made from pieces of hollowed out wood, lacking any kind of handle. From these pitchers they poured the drinks into similarly crafted small wooden cups, and the man whom Žarko referred to as host (though, at least to Vuk, the man seemed more an innkeeper) repeatedly rose to fetch new pitchers, changing out the empty ones. Most often fetched was wine, which Žarko immediately dove into. He right off rejected the cups as "too small" and instead grabbed one of the pitchers to drink from it. "A long time it has been since I drank a wine like this," commented over and over the cheered giant, upon whose cheeks now shone a visible blush, while his eyes had taken on a bit of a bloodshot look. In front of them, at the center of the table, on a gigantic wooden platter, piles of roasted and dried meat were laid – the guests followed the example of their hosts, taking pieces with their hands; there were no plates and no forks, and the one and only knife was stabbed into a large shoulder of roasted meat in the middle of the oval platter, in case it was needed. There was no bread, no cheese, no salt – nothing but meat on the table. But that meat, despite being unsalted, was truly delicious, and all ate it heartily. Vuk gave Senka a little piece of everything to taste, and it seemed that in those heaps and slabs were all sorts of known and unknown meats. They were soon stuffed without having tasted everything. At one point, Senka asked if a piece of meat could also be taken to her Vidra, so even the dog, who had stayed outside with the horse, thus shared in the royal meal.

The host did not allow any serious matters to be spoken of until the guests had eaten and drunk their fill. Till then, the only topic of discussion had been the quality of their drinks, made from "water from the heart of the earth," pulled up from a well located at the corner of the inn itself, along with endless rants on the best ways to dry or roast particular cuts of meat. Only when he felt that the guests had indeed been truly satiated, the host finally went into the topic of conversation which they all had eagerly awaited: "We rarely get a chance to listen to stories, which we love dearly. Thus, we would be gladdened to hear yours. You spoke of something troubling that was following you..."

And so, little by little, the usually very reserved Žarko recalled everything of importance which had happened to them over the last several days: the wine had obviously done its work and loosened his tongue. The men listened to him captivated, drinking in every word, exclaiming wonderment, approval, or excitement, which somehow always encouraged Žarko to speak on further. His story of encountering Senka started rather restrained, but as his narrative reached the rescuing of Vuk, he was already speaking in great detail, and by the time he got to describing the hellish wolves on their trail, he was almost exaggerating – he was so convincing that goosebumps broke out on the skin of Vuk, as if he himself had not been there to see that infernal pack. But the crippled thief remained as quiet as Senka, except now and again when a question was asked directly to him. Unlike Žarko, whose cheeks had grown more and more flushed as he had relaxed in drinking pitcher after pitcher, the thief and the girl were both still caught up in worries about their pursuers, as if they expected to hear the demonic howling in front of the door at any moment. But their hosts had obviously spoken rightly, comfortable in possessing a knowledge of which the guests could not be aware, as nothing disturbed the pleasant atmosphere of their feast. Or at least nothing but a subdued suspicion, probably fostered by concern, for Vuk had the constant feeling that these barefoot men were weighing him discreetly with their eyes, turning their heads aside whenever he would look to meet their prying gaze; he wondered if Senka had the same feeling, but did not want to spoil the pleasant atmosphere with unnecessary whispers, and so he never asked.

After hours of monologue, Žarko finally brought his tale to a close with his recount of the moment when he had seen the first cabin from within the stream they had been walking through. A hush then settled over the room. "And," the host was first to speak up, "what do you intend to do now?" "Well," answered Žarko, "I mean to wait here until morning, and to ask one of you, good people that you are, to lead us through these woods and out to the other side. Far from any path, and the closer to a town the better – if possible, one that is fortified. I believe that behind a walled town we might find a measure of security." After the warrior finished laying out this simple plan, a moment of silence held the air, while the villagers looked at one another, before all together bursting into a thunderous laugh. Žarko did not find this reaction pleasant – his eyes grew immediatly more bloodshot, while his voice took on somewhat of a grim, threatening tone: "I do not know what is funny, people. Are you laughing at Žarko?"

"Excuse us, warrior-Žarko, we mean not to offend you," replied the tavern's host calmly. "It is just that you do not know how things are in this place. As I told you earlier, time flows differently here – and that was not a lie. You would wait until morning, but that is not possible. For when you leave Morlak, in the forest you will find it to be the exact same time as when you entered. You are welcome here to rest and recover for as long as you like, even though I believe that you have found your freshness already, but morning is something that you cannot wait for." The man spoke all of this in a mild tone, almost as if explaining to a child some basic principles that are understood, and in which there is nothing strange to be found. "Also, you want one of us to take you out of the woods. And that also cannot be – none of us have ever left the borders of this forest, we do not know the way out of it. And to have found yourself here, this means you are lost in the woods, too – if you were to follow the stream backwards, you would never find the place where you entered it, as the water have erased your tracks and the forest have changed, so really you can only get out of it by chance, if you are to ever get out of here alive."

The bearded man finished, looking Žarko straight in the eye with no hint of deceit or mockery – or fear. The rising rage in Žarko retreated at the man's unusual words, and he could only mumble calmly: "So what then do we do, my host?" In the end it seems, they were indeed guests of a strange people, men who had welcomed them well and provided them comfort, and it would do no good nor be fitting to stir up trouble now: the practical side of Žarko's wine-slushed mind understood that they already had quite enough enemies. The host then spoke up again, still not turning aside his gaze: "The way out of the forest we know not, that is how things are. But we do know that in the middle of the woods rises a large mountain, where shepherds herd their sheep. They risk passage through our forest, for they say among themselves that on the slopes of that mountain is the finest pasture that can be found. They do know a way through the forest, and we Morlaks know the way to them. And would gladly guide you there."

– Chapter 13 –
Encounter Three

The party left Morlak with two new companions: the bearded innkeeper, who revealed that his name was Brado, and another man from the village, Vukan, who was somewhat shorter and slimmer than the other villagers, but who had journeyed most often to the shepherds. He said this as if it was worthy of praise.

Their guides remained barefoot even on this trek; without making a sound, they pressed gently across the forest floor, with steps as light as falling leaves. As they were departing, Vuk turned to look once more upon the strange village they were leaving behind. He was not surprised to see that the huts were once again shrouded in darkness, dimly lit only by the light of the full moon. He somehow expected it. All the men from the tavern, who had gathered on the edge of the village to bid them farewell, faded from sight, and not a hint of light could be seen from any of the huts.

So the column of travelers, now a few unshod figures longer, moved on. In front walked Vukan, the youngest of the Morlak men (or at least Vuk believed so), and behind him Žarko, who led the horse on which Senka and Vuk sat again, while Vidra followed along gracefully in their footsteps; fully at the rear was Brado, covering their tracks and removing any signs of their passing. The two Morlaks regarded this as necessary, since the group could no longer follow the stream that had helped to obscure their traces – the mountain to which they were heading was in a completely different direction. Brado assured them that he would erase their tracks to such a degree that after a few hours even wolves would not be able to follow them. For this purpose he used some shrubs, torn from their roots, which according to him were so strongly aromatic that in a short time the plants' fragrance would completely overwhelm any scent they left behind. He used these bushes to vigorously strike the ground here and there, along the route they walked, as if sweeping away with a broom some paths they traversed, while leaving others untouched, for reasons only his own. Yet, as no one else was well versed in erasing tracks, they were left to trust his methods.

When they drew away from the village, the silence of the night greeted them again, confirming what the Morlak men had spoken: outside the village it was still the dead of night, which had just begun. There were still many long hours until morning. Vuk marveled, however, over their feeling of being completely rested. Even though they had only managed to fortify themselves with food and drink, over just a few hours of sitting on relatively unforgiving wooden stools, he felt as if they were starting off after several nights of sleep. Vuk tapped Senka to ask, in a whisper, if she felt the same, and she was well rested too; there was indeed something very strange about the time in that village – still they could do nothing else but accept this as merely one of the many oddities that had befallen them these past days.

The two Morlaks estimated they would reach the mountain halfway through what remained of the night. And so it was: nothing unexpectedly dangerous occurred during their quiet venture forth, though danger was always looming above. They would now and again halt in the shadows of overhanging branches to hide from the view of the flying horde which continued to fly above the forest, searching for them, but they always managed to succeed, or so it seemed, in anticipating the arrival of the dusk imps by that characteristic unpleasant humming babble of shrieks and flaps. At one point, the imps flew so close that, from the shadows, fugitives could make out the flickering shine of the fires which sometimes burst from their mouths, lighting up just for an instant their sharp teeth and small yet foul bodies. They truly were a terrifying sight, even apart from the rest of the hellish retinue. As for the bloodthirsty howling, they heard it several more times, but each time it sounded further and further away. It looked as if they were indeed outwitting their tireless pursuers.

After a long and practically uninterrupted striding at a swift pace, during which they attempted to stay quiet, Vukan finally halted and turned to the others: "Just a bit ahead, and we arrive at the shepherd camp. It would be best if you come to the front now, and we will follow. And say nothing to the herders about our village. Tell them, Žarko, that we are all your servants. Seek escort to at least the edge of the forest, and see that you get it, and we will come along with you as far as we can." Without waiting for an answer, the smaller man went to the back of the column to join Brado. Žarko pulled on the loose reins of his horse, stepping forward, and thus they arrived at the foot of the mountain.

Vukan had led them to the right spot. As soon as they stepped past some thinning trees and out of the forest surrounding the mountain, a shepherd's camp appeared before them. It was impossible not to see it – unlike themselves, it was clear that the herdsmen were not hiding from anything. And why would they? It was a well-organized group of about thirty or so men that sat around a large, blazing fire placed in the center of the camp. Someone was speaking something obviously humorous, since the others frequently interrupted him with bursts of laughter. A good distance from the fire stood a single large tree, on whose branches the shepherds had things out to dry; several cloaks, shirts, and pants were hung about on all sides. Two shepherds were leaning against the tree, while the third one, likely serving as the lookout, was situated on some improvised platform in the tree branches; it was clear that they expected no danger, as this sentry was laughing along with the others, without ever taking his eyes off of the merry gang around the fire. Near the fire, several large tents were also set up, all of which were glowing dimly – apparently, there were fires lit inside as well, or at least some kind of torch or candle must have been kept burning in each. The tents were arranged in a closed semi-circular formation towards the woods, acting as a barrier before the mountain and a fence towards the clearing where an enormous herd of sheep lay in the grass, encircled by many dogs far larger than Vidra. By Žarko's quick estimation under the moonlight, the dogs seemed to vastly outnumber the shepherds, and many of them were awake, though only lazily watching the sheep. Their purpose now seemed more to guard the sheep from wandering away than from any approaching danger, as any significant threat for such a large group was unlikely. The dogs were certainly bred to be sheepdogs, and serious ones at that, concluded the warrior, who assumed that they likely even slept in shifts, just as watchmen would.

Taking all of this in, Žarko continued to advance his ragamuffin group towards the campfire. He had no intention to hide their arrival, but they did remain quiet. The herdsmen were so caught up in the entertaining story being told that the strange column had crossed nearly half the distance from the forest before they were noticed. First off, one of the closer dogs straightened his head, raising its ears and turning in the direction of the arriving party, then barked loudly. When the other dogs started baying as well, the watchman in the tree finally remembered his duty, raising his eyes to see what had set the dogs to barking. It was time for the newcomers to make themselves announced.

"Ahoy, herdsmen! May god grant you health!" shouted Žarko, loudly, but trying to refrain from being too loud, for he knew all the while that at any moment the scouting flying horde could be near. The noise around the fire died instantly and several of the men stood up and turned about to face them, while the rest remained sitting as they were by the fire, caught by surprise, cautiously peering out in the direction of the advancing bunch. Most of the herdsmen were unarmed, though some had knives hanging out of their belts, but all of them had their shepherd's crooks at hand; those who now stood leaned onto these sticks, each with a tip curved like a hook, and it was clear that they were useful for a number of things beyond catching sheep, and would make a good enough weapon in a pinch. None of the men responded to the greeting, so Žarko yelled out once more: "So is this the way that guests are greeted in a shepherds' camp?" To this finally came a reply from the man who had until that moment been holding court with his entertaining story: "Gods be with you, unknown travelers! What fortune leads you to us?"

"Not fortune, but misfortune, shepherds... wait a moment till we reach the fire and I will tell you of it!"

And soon the party found itself in the heart of the shepherds' camp. There was no time for pleasantries - the travelers refused food and drink, as well as to sit by the fire. Instead, they stood among the herdsmen, while Žarko narrated a shortened version of their story. This time there was no wine, so his sense of restraint had returned; he told them that they were being pursued by bandits, from whom they escaped to the forest only to become lost. And now here they were, his sister and servants, seeking help, seeking someone to guide them out of the woods. It did not appear that his story was particularly persuasive, as no immediate offers of help came forward. Perhaps shepherds were afraid of the bandits mentioned, or of the newcomers themselves, especially this giant of a man who spoke confidently of their troubles, but looked as if he had sent a good many to their ends himself. The shepherd who greeted them first was again the one to finally speak: "Yes, that is trouble, but we are not much help: each of us has his own obligations, and many are the sheep to watch over, we cannot spare even a single man..." But Žarko was not so easily dissuaded: "Shepherds, it is not the way, nor does it look well, to refuse help to a guest in need! And we need a guide to take us only to the forest's edge. Out of many, surely there is one man you could spare now, and that for a short while?!"

No, responded the shepherd, again answering similarly. They could spare no one, all of them must watch over the sheep. Little by little, anger at this unpleasantry had begun to overwhelm Žarko. And his patience did not need much to reach its end. He suddenly pulled a knife seemingly out of nowhere and threw it powerfully in the direction of the lone tree before anyone could react. Not a blink later, the blade, which had been hidden unseen in Žarko's belt-sheath, was now stuck deep in the tree trunk, just above the head of one of the men sitting under the tree. The terrified man looked up at the blade that was barely sticking out, as if swallowed by the old tree trunk, while Žarko roared in a thunderous voice: "Hear this, shepherds, from your guest in distress! The one who brings me back my knife does not have to travel with Žarko. And so help me God almighty, if none of you can, then you will all accompany us!" Silence followed. Vuk, who was still seated on the horse, could feel goosebumps rising up his spine in response. And he was in Žarko's party! He could only imagine how the herdsmen must have been feeling at that moment.

The stupefied group, mostly young lads, now found themselves truly in trouble. They looked at each other, but no one would speak a word. The one above whose head the knife had sung ventured first to pull it out – but he could not budge it even a hairbreadth. Then another sitting alongside pushed him away and tried, but with the same result – as if they were trying to pull the tree up by the roots. Two more shepherds tried, apparently known for their strength, but again to no avail. Then the man who had first spoken started to plead desperately, on the verge of panicked tears, realizing the situation he had put his fellows in: "Please, do not be like that, warrior, all gods be with you. I do not speak what I think, only what has been commanded to me; duties are determined by our chieftain, and we shepherds must obey!"

"Then where is this chieftain of yours? I have something to ask him!" thundered Žarko, so loudly it made even Senka and Vuk uncomfortable. Their protector was indeed strange in his ways, yet it was certainly better to be on his side of things. The pleading man answered in a quivering voice: "The chief is in his tent, that largest one, there. Maybe resting, or reading over a letter which arrived today from far away…"

The man had not yet finished speaking when, off to the right, came a voice, resonant and powerful, yet at the same time graceful and pleasant to the ear: "Here is the shepherd chief you seek, O warrior of an ancient ilk! Do not frighten my young shepherds so, rather tell me what is it you need." While saying this, the man was at the same time quickly heading for the lone tree, which he stopped in front of, and, with what looked like ease, pulled the knife out of the thick of the tree trunk. Then he turned and brought the knife to Žarko, holding the blade while offering the handgrip to its large owner, saying: "A good knife for a good warrior… better I have never seen!" The sudden change in the situation surprised everyone, including Žarko. Who was this vigorous man who could so easily pull the knife from the huge tree, the blade thrust in so deeply? He was dressed simply, just as the other shepherds, but larger, almost as massive as Žarko. He had a beautiful face, almost feminine, yet still manfully handsome, and an even more dashing stature, which not even his cumbersome cloak could hide – he was simply a pleasure to both look at and listen to.

Žarko accepted the knife by the handle, still thinking over what exactly to say (he was a bit confused by the final words of the chieftain – that ambiguous praise made unclear whether it was the knife he was admiring, or the warrior who carried it), when the man again spoke in his bell-clear voice: "I heard you rightly from the start, unknown warrior, but did not leave my tent right away as I was reading a small missive that came from afar. Though the letter is small, its trouble is large! By the will of gods, it seems, our paths are united – I as well must pass the forest, and do so as soon as I can. It will be my pleasure to guide you and make the journey with such an ally!"

Žarko was immediately pleased by what he heard, and so even answered quite politely, trying to emulate the refined style of the previous speaker: "Thank you, chieftain, for your help in time of trouble. Though you spend your time with sheep, you speak wisely, and act even more so; your manners would not shame me were we to stand before our king and his whole court! But tell me, if it be your will, how are you called, chieftain? By what name may Žarko call his brother in arms?"

"For my shepherd brotherhood here, I am Chieftain Miloš, but to you and whole your party, I will just be Miloš, brother, your fellow companion!"

And next, to the astonishment of all, the two men embraced brotherly. "At first sight," thought Vuk ironically, while all of them felt relieved that the unpleasant situation ended well. Fraternity had been offered, and accepted, making brethren out of the two possible opponents. The herdsmen began to cheer, and everyone relaxed. Miloš stepped back from Žarko, saying that he must bid farewell to his shepherds and issue them orders, after which they could immediately set forth upon their journey. And that is how it was – just a short while later, the strange bunch again ventured off into the forest, this time counting one more amongst its members, the one who should be their guide to safer pastures.

– Chapter 14 –
The Way of the Chieftain

Miloš and Žarko, nearly step for step, went together at the front of their column. Miloš led, and Žarko again retold their story, this time speaking the true version of the past days' happenings. He skipped over only the part about Morlak, even though Vuk, who could follow their conversation from the horse, was sure that even this would be told, as soon as the two

Morlak men accompanying them at the back of the column eventually left the party. Brado and Vukan were no longer attempting to conceal their tracks, since they were advancing too fast – Žarko hoped that they had already succeeded in losing their pursuers, and so he was against any additional slowing down. Miloš obviously knew the way well, for he led them along an unseen path as if it was made for passage, and they advanced at a quick pace, dictated by the pair at the forefront.

Miloš told Žarko that they would not make it out of the forest that morning, but rather by the following one, at best. "The way is long, my brother." And so it was agreed that they would push on without rest. It was remarkable watching how these two men spoke calmly, their voices barely louder than their footsteps, while at the same time leading the column forward through the woods at almost a run. Vuk realized that Miloš, in some inexplicable way, seemed to bring out the best in Žarko. For the most part sullen and grumbling, the warrior now moved with an agility which earlier he had not seemed to possess, all the while talking in the most pleasant and cordial way. It was simply hard to believe that this was the same man who, just a bit before, had almost caused a scuffle in the herding camp. Vuk realized how glad he was that this Miloš was with them, and hoped that it would last as long as possible.

Žarko asked their guide directly where he was going and why. After a barely noticeable hesitation, Miloš answered: "I am going to the town of Vučitrn, but do not ask my why. I can only say that I am pulled by what is strongest in this world: even a shepherd, free in the forest, cannot resist the love of his dearest." He added that he would later tell him more, once they exited the forest and escaped from the evil following them. The shepherd chieftain was now fully aware of the enormity of their danger, yet seemed neither disturbed, nor frightened – Vuk felt certain that he would accompany them regardless of the threat. Žarko suggested that, when they succeeded in emerging from the forest, they should go with him to Vučitrn as well: for quite awhile he had been thinking that behind a town's fortifications they would be secure from that which hounded them. Miloš agreed wholeheartedly.

There was something very similar about the way these two carried themselves – even if Žarko was a good deal rougher, they still spoke and moved alike, and appeared to understand each other perfectly. There were not too many questions in their discussions. As if two long lost brothers had suddenly found one another, they seemed to possess an understanding that went beyond words. In another situation, this might have made Vuk think deeper, but his mind was now more than occupied with worry over their pursuers; he often looked back or up at the sky through the branches, trying to spot any sign of oncoming danger. He also asked Senka to inform him when or if she heard anything suspicious – he realized that the girl now fully relied on her sense of hearing, and that this should not be underestimated: even he, who was not blind, could hear better after keeping his eyes closed for some time, and this had become apparent to him over many of his nighttime ventures in thievery. He thought, marveling for a moment, how human nature had ways of sharpening other senses at the expense of the missing ones, and with that again directed his gaze upward into the sky.

And as for Senka, she was lost in her own thoughts. While listening to Žarko's tale once again and, as part of it, his brief overview of the small, uninteresting life that was hers until just a few days ago, she began to grasp the grand scale of the adventure she now found herself in. Žarko managed to condense all that happened to her prior to the burning house into just a few brief sentences, while his recounting of the few following days could stretch for hours. She also pondered over how the group of people around her seemed to grow by the hour. And what did she know, really, about these people? Absolutely nothing – she was travelling with a bunch of strangers, whose lives were a mystery to her. Of Žarko she knew nearly as little as when she first met him; even though she had spoken much with Vuk, their conversation had never hit upon his past, so she could say the same for him; and now here was this Miloš, at first impression irresistibly composed, and yet again just one more about whom she would likely not be able to say a thing – while as for the "Morlaks," these men were an unexplainable mystery not only to her but for all, a riddle beyond her imagination. She wondered if the others were thinking over such things, this essential unknowing of their own companions, but then, with almost the skill of the greatest philosophers who she also knew nothing about, concluded that this is perhaps always the way, and it did no good to think too hard over it.

In their rapid journey they were soon greeted by the morning. From the moment that Miloš had joined them, they had not once come across a fly-by of the imp scouts. Were they moving faster than their enemy assumed? Was it possible that they had succeeded in somehow escaping the black menace? Yet it was now, with the coming of morning, that Miloš for the first time seemed concerned, but for another reason. He was just telling Žarko that this day they would be coming to the most dangerous part of their journey. The section ahead was the reason that no one, excepting him and his shepherds, ever attempted to lead their sheep to the greener pastures at the foot of the mountain in the middle of the forest. It was a hazardous area in which it was often possible to encounter a being of the wilderness which all men would do good to avoid – Lesnik, the lord of the forest himself.

"It is said that he may be encountered everywhere, for every forest is his kingdom. Yet it seems, just as any shepherd, that he also has his favored nooks and vales: we have come across him twice in the area that lies ahead. I would rather not speak of it now, but heed my words: we barely weathered that storm alive. And therefore I would recommend..."

And so the party accepted the strange measures of protection which Miloš went on to suggest: they halted briefly, while all but Senka took off their upper layers of clothes and turned them backwards, doing similarly with their shoes, so that on their left feet they wore those that would normally be worn on the right. Then they continued their journey, with their company now looking truly odd indeed: it was quite a ridiculous sight to see these giant men with their vests spread open on the back, while the higher back parts now rose up to the front middle of their necks, nearly strangling them. Even more so, contrary to the Morlaks, Žarko and Miloš were visibly hampered by the wrong foot shoes that constricted them, while the chieftain's otherwise cumbersome cloak now made him look like a bear walking about on two legs. All of this of course significantly impeded the progress of their march. The men of Morlak suffered it best – they were at least barefoot, so they still moved through the woods with a silent grace. Vuk and Senka, seated on the horse, were also spared from the worst of the discomfort of their switched over shoes.

Žarko, whose behavior until then had been a model of restraint, now began to sour: "We have listened, brother Miloš, and did as you asked, without hesitation. But tell me this frankly, please: are you fooling with us out of spite?" And again Miloš had an appropriate response for Žarko. He laughed out loud, from the heart, not minding the danger, then said: "God above us as my witness, Žarko, out of malice I would not torment you, that much should be clear. Only madmen would mock thusly! I am not playing you for fools, but must insist again that this is the best and perhaps the only safeguard." Their guide then went on to explain how Lesnik could not see travelers dressed up in such an incongruous way, or perhaps he did not care to see them; ever since the shepherds had begun to dress oddly as they passed through these woods, they had stopped encountering the lord of the forest.

Despite their earlier agreement to make no breaks, they now had to: Žarko would simply stomp to a halt whenever it became too much for him to take another step, and the others had but little choice than to follow his example, waiting for him to show his intent to move on again. His already familiar boorish behaviour returned in full, and everyone had to put up with it, yet Miloš simply guided them on as best he could, without paying it any mind.

– Chapter 15 –
Encounter Four

And this awkward column was proceeding just so when it came across the maiden. There she was, sitting on a slight rise in the ground, right in the middle of the imaginary path they intended to follow. As if she was waiting for them. They saw her from afar, and she had seen them too, yet she still did not move in the slightest, nor show any worry or surprise. She just continued to sit, watching as they approached with their ungainly footsteps.

A maiden in the middle of the forest. She was quite a young woman, likely not more than twice the age of Senka. Yet the full bloom of her womanhood could not be hidden even under the shabby mantle she wore – and she was indeed dressed like some old woman: all in black, in a long simple dress of the most basic stitching that reached her ankles, but seemed constricting in its upper sections, visibly emphasizing even further the generous curve of her bosom; hanging over her shoulders was a long black cloak sloping all the way down to the ground, if not even dragging along the forest floor – it now fell in soft folds all around her upon the slight mound where she sat. A dark scarf partly concealed her lush and wild hair, but waves of it billowed out on all sides, spilling over her back and chest. Across her knee she held a wooden staff, long like the shepherd's crook on which Miloš now leaned, yet finer, and carved for its entire length, curving at the top like a snake, with red stones inlaid like eyes on both sides. But most striking of all were her eyes: cheerful and mocking, they shifted ceaselessly from one traveler to another, and while they were approaching it was obvious that she was ridiculing them without a single spoken word. The travelers themselves were so surprised by this unlikely encounter in the forest that they had not shared a word with each other either – they just stared as if bewitched at this apparition of a girl in front of them, continuing to advance towards her, so that Senka remained unaware of this new presence until the maiden herself spoke up when they came very close:

"I have yet to see such a bunch! From a buffoon to a loony, a shepherd for wolves, the blind, and the lame."

As a response, she was greeted by complete silence. Even the ever-ready warriors at the front of the column seemed surprised by the girl's audacity. Vuk once again felt the ever more frequent creep of goosebumps up his back, followed by uneasiness; how could she know that he was a cripple if he was sitting on the back of a horse? And how could she know his name, if in mentioning wolves she had really meant him? That was possible, as his name was the same as for any wolf in these woods! It was somewhat obvious to assume that Miloš was a shepherd, but then again... how could she have guessed that Senka was blind? The young girl always had her eyes open and her gaze on the ground, as if she was constantly ashamed, so that even Vuk did not immediately recognize her blindness when they first met. Or perhaps the young woman had thought of them differently – the "lame" could just as well mean Žarko and Miloš, as they were limping with their shoes on the wrong feet...

"What is with you, unsung heroes? Should I speak backwards so that you might understand? Shall I turn around so you can see me?"

"I know not who you are, little piss-ant wench, but nobody talks like that to Žarko!" roared the giant, stepping towards her, but Miloš held him back: "Hold on a moment, brother! Surely you do not mean to beat a girl?

Yes, it would be easy with arms, but let us try first with words..." Žarko stopped at Miloš's prudent comments, but the girl continued as if she had no intention of relenting with her provocations.

"And thus speaks the great and the wise Miloš... it is my honor to meet you, O chief of the shepherds. And what caused you to split from your sheep? Have you, like your ewes, decided to follow the most headstrong ram of them all?"

Now it was Miloš's turn to be offended, yet he instead answered in a calm voice, bell-like as always, but now with a noticeable dose of sarcasm, on par with girl's own: "My brother here might be like a ram, yes, a battering ram that breaks things. And no sheep can outrun his horns, girl, so think closely what you say hereafter – I have held Žarko back once, but I shall not do so again! Now tell me forthwith – how is it that you know of me?"

These words seemed to shatter the young woman's desire for further conflict. Abruptly, her voice gained a depth well beyond her years, at the same time ridding itself of any hint of sarcasm.

"I know about you, Miloš, that is true. And I know about the others, too: I know of the hero Žarko, of the cripple Vuk, of the blind girl Senka and of her dog Vidra. I know even of the two barefoots at the rear, and much more than you do, or any other member of your fellowship. But where do I know this from, that I am not going to say! It is up to you as to whether will you trust me, for I wish to travel with you." Just like that, she had laid it all – and all of them – bare. An almost tangible confusion now seized the pack of travelers. Who was this girl who knew their names, and beyond that, she now even wished to join them?!

"Hold it right there, mad-headed woman! To our questions you answer with secrets, and you want our trust? Why accept such a stranger into our companionship? You could be a spy or a scoundrel, or even a witch – such knowledge as you possess does not come to just anyone."

After Miloš spoke these words, silence followed, while the two disputants held each other's eyes, unblinking. Miloš had said all he had in that clear, calm, bell-like voice, lowering the tension just as the young woman herself, but still the weight of his insinuations reached the heart of each of his companions. It appeared that the woman was also aware of this, and that she was stewing over how to respond, though her face showed no sign of emotion. After a tense, overlong moment, she spoke once more.

"You are indeed wise, shepherd Miloš, even wiser than they say. Not a witch, that I am not – yet. But I am indeed a mora; daughter of the greatest witch of them all. And though I have not yet assumed the powers that await me in my womanly maturity, I am capable of seeing things that neither you nor others can; so you all should listen to what I am about to say: your fellowship is not unforeseen. It has not come together by chance. Each of you have a quest, bestowed upon you by the gods themselves. Some of you hide yours willingly, while others know not yet what theirs are. And I have my own to fulfill: to see all your quests accomplished. About all of you I have dreamt for years… now we meet and I have revealed myself, though I could have used deception to enter your party. Think over this further if you must, for I shall say no more – already I have said too much! Let me go along with you, I will not get in the way; and if you suspect my motives, I will at least be at hand's reach."

Saying this, the young woman dropped her gaze, as if surrendering to the decision of the party. Miloš thought briefly, then looked inquiringly towards Žarko, who gazed back, then sternly nodded his head in consent. The two had understood one another without a word exchanged, recognizing the truth to the girl's claims; whoever she was, she would not hamper them much, and it would be wise to keep her close, as she already knew more than one should. So Miloš spoke: "Let it be then, new companion! Go behind the horse and follow, but not quite in the back – I want to not worry over whether you will leave traces for someone – or something. And say also, before we set off, how shall we call you?"

The young woman raised her head. Her face glowed with an irrepressible joy – if she was pretending, she did so very convincingly. Perhaps she herself had not believed that she would succeed in joining the party, though her next words allayed any such doubts: "Marena is my name, but you can call me Mara, similar to the mora that I am… and thank you for accepting me, even though it was inevitable." Saying this, she finally stood up from the elevated spot where she was sitting all through their exchange, and with quick steps strode across, taking her spot just behind the horse. The beauty of her movement struck everyone in the companionship, even more so the grace with which she moved despite the cumbersome dress and cloak, as well as the way each of her movements augmented her womanly form even under such unfeminine attire. After watching mora's elegant glide in fascination, the now even longer column continued on its way. Žarko or Miloš would now and again look back in mistrust to see what their new companion was up to, but she only followed the horse with unbroken steadfastness, looking at the ground in front of her, as if completely lost in her thoughts.

– Chapter 16 –
Mara, Daughter of a Witch

Vuk did not feel right with this mysterious girl walking just behind his back. She did not inspire his trust, and if he had been the one to decide, she never would have joined them. But no one had asked him – the decision belonged to Žarko and Miloš. As for Senka, she was not sure what she felt. On the one hand, she was somewhat cheered that she was no longer the only female member of the group, but on the other, this young woman made her feel oddly uneasy. She felt that very little could be kept hidden from her, and it was not a pleasant feeling, even for a little girl with not much to hide.

From the moment she had joined their companionship, Marena was silent, not sharing a single word with anyone since their initial conversation. But perhaps it was better this way, since everyone in the party remained anxious about her presence, excepting perhaps the two men in front. The daughter of a witch! All of them knew, if only from stories, that such a child was destined to become a witch herself, and from very early on would have begun to learn the "craft" of witchcraft, from which it seemed no good could come. And Mara made no attempt to hide this; had she not said herself that she was the daughter of the greatest of witches, something still reverberating upsettingly between each of the party's ears? So, consciously or unconsciously, they all kept their distance from her as best they could.

"I had just found some relief in the passing of night, and look now, a whole new trouble to worry over..." thought Vuk, and the others likely had similar thoughts. The weight of Marena's presence among them had pushed from their heads everything else she had spoken of, even though those weighty implications demanded serious consideration. They all acted in accordance with the age-old belief that a witch cannot be trusted under any terms (even if this one was a mere mora who had revealed that she had not yet achieved full witchhood). As for the other ominous matters, they were more than willing to forget them all for a while and simply worry over the one and only thing she had let be known about herself.

The day slunk by in a mood of gloom – the relief of having survived the night was replaced by a witching discomfort, made worse by the constant grumpiness of Žarko, still grunting over his swapped-about shoes. This giant, who just hours earlier had been ready to single-handedly fight the entire demonic army, now behaved as if this trip was the greatest torture imaginable. If not for Miloš, he would have long ago given up on this nonsense and dressed himself back as one is intended to be; only Miloš's disquiet whenever he would mention doing such a thing kept him in a semblance of belief that this whole mess of switching things around – and making fools of themselves in the process – could somehow indeed save them from some unseen peril.

It was almost evening, and already for the tenth time they had halted because of the warrior, when Mara spoke up for the first time as a member of the party: "You can now end your bizarre disguise. That danger has passed." Miloš looked back at her sharply: "How do you know this, companion?"

She answered him gently, as if clarifying something that should have been already understood. "I know much, my lord Miloš, even if I know not how, or from where this knowledge comes. Just as I know that you are dressed backwards because of the danger that is the lord of the forest, and not so you would look like a bungled troupe of fools to any one you might come across, I know too that this danger has passed. And I know what it is that is following you…" And here Marena stopped, making it tantalizingly clear that she would not talk any further if they were not interested in hearing her out.

At this, Žarko suddenly jumped into the conversation, already too fed up to suffer Mara's ambiguities: "Speak up, woman, and speak now, so that Žarko does not open your mouth for you!"

"If you so insist, Žarko… this fellowship, so now me as well, is being followed by something utterly impure… and evil… It is something that you must have all heard of, and surely considered sinister and horrific, but the one that is following us is much more than just this… if creatures such as these roam the black places of the earth, dark and lifeless, preying on the living, then this one is their undisputed lord. There is no other way for me to say it, though my tongue repels – the foul thing in question is nothing other than… a vampire!" Having said this, the young woman already knew what scornful reaction would follow. Žarko raised an eyebrow in a pose of mocking disbelief, while Miloš smiled down at her like a child speaking nonsense; nonetheless, she continued, unwavering: "Yes, a vampire… look at me as you will, but that is exactly what it is. And it is not just any vampire – what follows us is the Nightlord, with his army; before his untimely death, the greatest of warriors, yet revived as a dark servant of the most foul forces many years after his fall. Unusual for a vampire, as even any villager knows that a man can be vampired only within the first forty days after his death, but that does not hold true for this one... Perhaps centuries passed from the time of his death before he was reborn – in darkness. And as far as I know, it has been ages since such things have existed in the realms of men. For devils such as these, it is said, in contrast to other vampires, they sleep not even during the day, and they can even bring others to darkness themselves..."

"Wench, stop with such nonsense!" interrupted Žarko, shouting at her. "Even if there ever were such beings, even a child knows vampires are only to be feared at night - by daylight it is impossible to come across one!"

"You think so, Žarko? I know you have wondered at why that dark horseman – and see here, I know indeed that it is a horseman! – did not attack you upon your first encounter. Think again why it is so..." Žarko's gloomy look spurred her to get to the point quickly, as this was no time for riddles: "It was still day! His strength then is far from its peak, which he does not reach until the dead of night, and which holds until the first flickers of morning. Remember that cloaking swarm of imps? Their role is not only to serve as scouts – no, they serve an even more sinister purpose: they create night for their lord even while the day lives! Think well over this, then tell me again that it is impossible..."

And this time Žarko did think it over. And while he did not believe any of it, he could not deny the countless oddities and wonders that had come upon them in this short time – why would a vampire not be yet another? "It is not that I believe you, witch," he finally grumbled, "but there is one thing that concerns me: can such a thing be killed? By blade, or mace, or battle spear?"

Mara had been awaiting just such a question: "He is unnaturally strong and almost invincible, but yes, he can indeed be killed, just as any vampire might be: the most opportune way would be to pierce his heart with a wooden stake, best if made from hawthorn, but by the looks of it, your spear would likely serve well enough. The other way is more difficult: his head needs to be cut off, but he must be beheaded so completely that every last scrap of skin is detached from the rest of his body, otherwise the vampire will put his head back on and escape, and with time the head will coalesce with the body once again. It is probably safest to do both things, and then burn the corpse – only that can guarantee that an ancient vampire of this sort will never return to torment this world again. That is, unless his soul escapes before this is done, which one should not allow."

A grave silence followed, as all of them puzzled over what they had just heard. Some with fear, others with disbelief, and some still thinking over the hidden intentions this unusual young woman held. Miloš was the first to bring forward a new question: "As you seem to know such secrets, is there more that you would care to share?"

Mara looked him back straight in the eyes, aware of the distrust. "Since you ask so graciously, my lord Miloš, then I will tell you so: I know that we could rest right here until the dead of night, because we face no imminent danger, but I would not suggest that, since I fear that you might think that I am up to something wicked…"

This left Miloš in bit of a bind, unsure of what to do next. He could see that Žarko was at the edge of his patience, tired and unwilling. And he knew that, after so much strenuous pushing to get to where they were now, they were still nowhere close to exiting the forest before dawn. While he thought on, he saw that Žarko had already started switching his shoes back to normal, as Mara had suggested. "Since it seems we have a witch with us, we might as well listen to her once in a while…" grumbled the brute, somewhat embarrassed (or at least as close as to embarrassed as he could be) by the disappointed look of his brotherly companion. Miloš, at this, relented: "Very well, Žarko, if you say so, then let us listen to her fully on this! We are more than exhausted – some rest would do us good." And so the company decided that right there on the spot, in the middle of the forest, they would rest until the approach of midnight.

Vuk volunteered to take the watch. "One does not get so tired on the back of a horse, and the rest of you have been on foot for a long while, so I will take the vigil." No one had anything against this. "The females sleep beside the tree, and we men around them. So if something visits, let it meet the warriors first!" With these sparse words, Žarko had set the sleeping arrangement, and all of them could hardly wait to lay down on the ground. Senka curled up against Vidra on one side and kept her other side as far as she could from Marena. The horse was let loose to roam about and graze, trusting that Vuk would stop it if it were to wander too far afoot. The sun had yet to fully set, and already the entire companionship, save for the watchman, was fast asleep. After half of a night and a whole day of slogging, the rest was indeed hard-earned.

Before midnight, they were awoken by Vuk. By the moon's position, it was clear that the dead of night was not far off. First Miloš, then Senka, then Brado and Vukan were shaken from their sleep. When Vuk got to Marena, he hesitated a moment, but then she awoke just as he leaned over her. In moments, all of them were already up on their feet, except for Žarko, whose snoring continued. For who would dare wake him? Moody after shaking off sleep, he might kill someone just in banishing the evils of his dreams...

Who else then, but Miloš. He shouted over to him, from afar: "Have you rested, Žarko? It is a hard day's night ahead of us..."

Žarko startled from his sleep, snorted through his nose once so hard that it looked like his mustache might fall off, and grunted: "I have not slept a wink! At all! I could not breathe, it felt like drowning, darkness like a nightmare straddling and pressing down upon me..."

"A nightmare? Surely a mora pressed upon you, since you had not pressed against her! You know what they say, greedy as a mora on a young fellow..." a mocking voice answered from behind him. At this, Žarko jumped, still sleepy, yet already grumpy, but when he saw Mara standing there with a mischievous little smile, he let his anger go. "Damn you, you wicked witchy-wench!" he raised his voice at her a little, succeeding even to smile harshly, only to turn it into a grimace a moment later when he, with a muffled cursing and a quick brush of his hand, knocked to the ground a ladybug which had carelessly settled on his neck. The young woman again smiled jeeringly: "Do not curse the bug that brings you luck… as she is a lady like me!"

Soon the group had gathered itself and resumed their march, finally dressed more fittingly. As they went, Žarko and Miloš asked Vuk if anything out of the ordinary had happened during their sleep. "Nothing whatsoever…" he told them. There had been no sound of hellish wolves, nor imps, nor any other unnatural forces. He was still saying so when, without warning, a lone long menacing howl broke the night's silence! Like an anguished cry, but this time much closer than it had been the night before. Too close. Everyone froze in their place, only to hear a number of other wolves' voices wail back, as if answering, and all of these as if they were just behind them.

"Get moving, folks, trouble is upon us!" hissed Žarko. And with this they immediately began rushing forward, moving as swiftly as they could while trying to make as little noise as possible. He spun a look at Mara: "We are safe until the dead of night! Is that what you said, damn witch's daughter?" She answered him, also in a pressed whisper, as quickly as she could in this rush: "And have I misled you, Žarko? Did any danger come to us thus far? What I knew, I spoke – but now midnight approaches, and danger with it!" Žarko did not seem convinced: "Ahh, you tramp, you tricked us... while we rested, the enemy overtook us! Safe until the dead of night, my ass – we are more likely dead this night! By gods, if the going gets tough, your head will be the first to fly!" He then doubled his pace to join Miloš at the head of the column.

"Where to, my Miloš? Do we have a chance, can we get away?"

"You are asking, Žarko, of our chances? I would not bet a single sheep on us!"

At this, Žarko ruefully let a sour smile, then spoke again: "Well then where do we go, brother? If we are to lose our heads, I would rather take off a few of the enemies' than have them get us at our backs, slaughtering us one by one…"

"Just run onward, warrior! A short ways ahead is a small rise, half of it ringed by thick brambles of poisonous thorns. If we make it to there, that would be a good place to make a stand; then we shall turn any way you want, and fight as you wish!"

The agonizing pursuit raged on. Behind them they could hear the constant howling closing in, and soon from a distance that terrible whirling of shrieks and wingbeats began to ring in their ears. On top of the night's darkness, a more eerie blackness was coming for them. A chill began to stab at their hearts no matter the hot sweat pouring down their skin. Yet on and on they pressed, fleeing in a dash without stopping. None of the fugitives could say how long this chase was lasting – it seemed as if they were running forever, or at least a whole night's length. Sapped and ever short of breath, they wished simply to collapse to the stony earth, but their instinct to survive spurred them forward in a race for their lives. Finally, they arrived.

When they at last gained the ground which Miloš had marked for their final stand, they were soaked through with sweat and battered from their scrambling. Even Senka and Vuk, who only had clung to the horse's back during their desperate exertion, were covered in scratches and breathing heavily. Yet fear remained stronger than exhaustion, and the chased party quickly turned about on this small knoll, no higher than a man, surveying their lot and trying to determine the best position for confronting the adversaries close on their heels.

The rise they found themselves stranded on was nothing more than a small forest slope, gradually rising to its highest point, where stood a huge tree with magnificent branches, somehow offset from the rest of the surrounding forest. Around the tree, all along the semicircular elevation, the ground was swept bare, covered only by short, stubbly grass, while closing the full circle on the backside was a thick patch of thorny briar, just shorter than a man, which covered the remainder of the rise, crawling toward the tree, gnarling about it densely in closer proximity than the rest of the forest. They had to admit that, given their circumstances, Miloš could not have chosen a better place, with a wall of poisonous thorns to guard their backs, though he warned them to remain aware of the thorns and not get too close, even in the thick of the fight, for he had already lost one shepherd to their sting. Upon Žarko's quick approval, Miloš related that the shepherds had come across this spot once while making their passage through the woods, and from then on used it as a place to make camp – the small clearing provided enough grazing for the sheep, while the thorns made for ample protection on the one side, so that just one man could watch over the entire flock. And, as if confirming his words, the companions noticed the remnants of a campfire near the large tree. "It is a pity that we will hardly live long enough to relight that fire ourselves," thought Vuk grimly, though he kept these thoughts to himself.

Žarko, clearly the most experienced in combat among the party, took upon himself the organization of their defense. Women were to remain in the rear, beside the enormous trunk of the tree. Žarko told them to climb into the tree if things turned for the worse, but until then to sit tight against the trunk and rest – the dusk imps would have a hard time seeing them under the cover of the thickest clumps of branches. As soon as Senka sat, Vidra curled up against her legs. The horse was tied to a low, thick branch, quite close to the thickets of thorns, but not so close that it could scratch itself upon them if frightened. The men were also instructed to stay within the range of the tree, while Žarko laid out the strategy in the case an attack penetrated. He and Miloš would attempt to hold the exposed center and the right flank, for, as the warrior commented: "Anything that can get through Žarko and Miloš will be very difficult for any man to handle." Vuk,

Brado, and Vukan were given the joint task, to the best of their abilities, of defending against anything that made it through on the left and of blocking the approach to the tree, protecting the women at all costs.

– Chapter 17 –
Weapons and Chanting

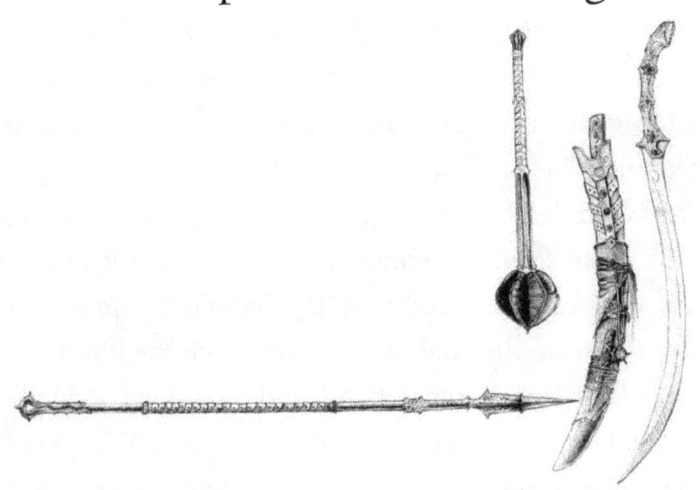

The burly warrior grunted his serious dissatisfaction over the weapons they had at their disposal: Vuk had absolutely nothing – the villagers who had wanted to take off his hand had never given him back his knife; Vukan also had nothing, while Brado had a small knife about his belt, more suitable for cutting forest plants than heads; Miloš had only his hunting knife and his hefty shepherd's crook; Senka was not only blind, but also unarmed, while Mara had her strange, carved staff, similar to Miloš's, though the women were not regarded by the men as serious potential combatants. Žarko swore hotly. Only he, a hardened fighter, was armed for two.

"Miloš, brother, do you want a sabre, if you know how to wield one?" he asked after a little hesitation, "For I will have enough weapons with my mace and battle spear and the hidden snake knife in my belt!"

Miloš smiled. "Gladly, brother, and I shall not disappoint you: I know how to cut both heads and branches! We can tally, if the battle lasts, which weapon will bring down more: your heavy mace or your sharp-edged saber."

Žarko smiled back through his thick whiskers, pulling out his sabre from the scabbard and throwing it over to Miloš, who caught it deftly by the handle, made several slicing flourishes through the air, then took the blunt side of the blade by his other hand and examined it in the moonlight: "This is a fine saber, Žarko… a magnificent one even – I have never held a better weapon! And such a unique blade…"

The warrior responded: "The sabre was a gift, my Miloš, earned for arduous valor in aid to a king whom I do not serve. On it are three hilts of gold, each one with a precious stone; the blade can slice right through other swords, it is worth more than three kingly cities… And if we survive this battle, or even if we fall, that sabre is yours, my brother!"

At that, the shepherd chieftain quickly looked back at him and again the two men understood one another beyond words. Miloš hid his tearful eye, only nodding slightly, and they continued with preparations for battle. The shepherd chieftain gave his staff to Vuk and handed his knife over to Vukan, who strangely refused it, saying that he could handle himself without it; Miloš shrugged his shoulders, and then bent down to Senka, putting the dagger in her hands and saying: "May the grace of your gods allow this to stay unneeded, but hold it tight, for evil is nigh." In the meantime, Žarko unclasped his battle spear from his back, took it in his left hand and then leant on it, while in his right he held his heavy battlemace, letting it sway lightly in the air. Miloš stepped over and stood beside him, resting his sword against his right leg while looking over all that lay before them. They were as ready as they could be.

And so the company braced themselves for the looming battle and the overwhelming odds against them. They stood in silence, swathed in the shadows of the ancient tree, anxiously awaiting that which was bound to come. No one thought about the outcome; their uneasiness did not stem from the likely defeat, but from the suspense of waiting – their options were expired, and now all that remained was that which the gods had set at them, and they thought only of how best to meet it. It was not the first time that Žarko found himself in such an inescapable position – very likely the same was also true for Miloš – and the others observed their demeanor and took it on as their own. Being brave is not about being without fear, but mastering that fear. And in the company of heroes, even the most modest of souls may become one.

The howling was becoming louder and louder. By the directions from which the voices whined out, it seemed as if the wolves were setting a noose about them and slowly pulling it tighter. Then the first three hellish beasts appeared. Demonic, for it would be hard to imagine a more apt description – their eyes shown through the darkness in a red, blood-tinted glow; it was these eyes that could be made out far before the beasts themselves broke out of the forest cover, and the black, long shapes of their bodies raged onto the grassy soil. The horse felt their presence and began rearing, neighing, and turning about in its spot, while Senka, from Vidra's raised hair and constant muffled growl, knew indeed that trouble was finally upon them.

While the howling continued to echo from the distance around them, these first three creatures attacked them without a sound. Žarko reckoned that these wolves were much larger than any he had ever come across or heard of before, but then, without wasting further thought, stepped forward quickly to engage the closest one at the front. With unbelievable precision, he threw his battle spear directly into the open growling jaws of the first wolf. With that, he bounded in the direction of the second, closing the space between them in two quick, long steps, and then brought the heavy end of his mace crashing down on its skull between the ears, stopping the beast in the place, with its head planted in the grass. Miloš held his own as well: quickly charging the third wolf, which jumped at him in a full run, the shepherd deftly stepped to the side, dodging the attack, and sliced across the wolf's neck with his saber, almost completely severing the creature's head from its body.

Both heroes looked around, but these were the only three attackers. Žarko rushed over and with a strong tug pulled his spear from the first corpse, then quickly retreated back under the tree's cover. "Well, there it is… they have found us!" Vuk muttered, giving grim voice to what was clearly known to them all by the circle of howls pulling tight about them, so close that their eyes now darted around, trying to catch a glimpse of the invaders. Žarko, however, was now in a much better mood – the waiting and running was finally over and he could, at last, fight! "I am not sure if you are counting, my brother, who of us is ahead thus far in the battle?" he snorted to Miloš through his thick mustaches. "But it is still early, and I am still only getting used to my new saber…" responded the shepherd with a wide smile. Their attention, however, was then drawn over to the muffled murmur of the men of Morlak, who were urgently articulating something to Vuk as he stood leaning on Miloš's staff…

… but all of this was suddenly interrupted by a horrible shriek that curdled the blood in each of the companion's veins! There was nothing human in that screech, yet they knew that it could not have come from the throat of a wolf, nor from the dusk imps. It was a powerful, high, sharp, resounding scream. It ripped through the night air like an arrow, with such force that their ears pained with its echoes, even though it seemed still far off. And it must have been some kind of command, for right afterwards the forest fell into silence, and only after that silence lingered awhile did the trapped party again hear the spine-chilling whirring of wings steadily approaching from a distance. And through the forest's undergrowth, like hundreds of flickering candles, pairs and pairs of red eyes began to appear… The creatures above and below were gathering at the edge of the small clearing, still unwilling to emerge. Soon they were entirely surrounded by a legion of eyes staring at them from the dark.

"Do we have a shred of hope left against this many?" Žarko turned to Miloš. "I do not know, Žarko, it does not look good, but we will not give our heads away lightly!"

In that uneasy quiet that hung in the air as they awaited the impending attack, all of the companions' ears were again drawn to the strange, agitated chant-like conversation which the Morlak men pressed on with, in urgent whispers, all directed at the cripple leaning on a stick.

"Remember, Vuk, remember who you are…"

And this conversation which had started in whispers was slowly but surely turning into a loud argument, with the men of Morlak now almost chanting rather than talking.

"Remember, Vuk, who you are, we beg of you!"

"I do not know, men, what you are talking about..."

"Remember, Vuk! If you are the one, you must remember!"

"What?! I do not understand you!"

"Remember, lame wolf, your true self! The prophecy of your arrival is as old as Morlak – Remember who you are!"

"Enough, men, let off! What to remember? You make no sense!"

"Remember yourself, lame wolf! Your arrival is foretold – that you would come with strange friends, and that you still would not know!"

"Know what?! And who could know of our arrival? Whoever told you this nonsense, it certainly was not about me!"

"It is foretold that you would not know, but that, when danger threatens, you will remember. Remember who you are!"

"Men, I cannot say it any clearer – I know not what you are talking about and have nothing to recall!"

It was obvious that Vuk felt more and more exasperated with the incessant onrush of words the two barefoot men set at him, their badgering only increasing in intensity at this worst of times. Then, without warning, one of the two men from Morlak suddenly grabbed the cripple's shirt with both hands and ripped it open. Moonlight exposed his shaggy chest, at the same time revealing something curious on the side, high up on the left of his breast: a striking black mark could be made out there, in a shape most similar to a wolf's head. But only for a moment, before Vuk let out an upset snarl, dropping the stick to use both hands to pull his now torn shirt back across his torso. "Are you crazy?!" he mufflingly yelled. The two men pulled back, their faces lit with wonder.

"It truly is you, leader of the pack!" The voices of Morlak men exclaimed together in one breath, now overcome with awe, though finally maintaining a small distance from the limping man. "You came with strange friends, and lame, not knowing yourself, and here is the mark etched on your chest!"

"People, for your god's sake... that is not some drawing on my chest, it is but a birthmark. By that shape I was named Vuk, a lone wolf!"

"That is as it should be! It is said that this mark of the chieftain is the sign we draw upon our chest. Remember who you are, leader!"

They then both pulled their vests open, under which they wore nothing, each revealing that just to the left and high up on their upper left breast, in precisely the same spot as Vuk, they were marked with the exact same sign. This at once both jolted and confused the lame thief, who remained momentarily wonderstruck.

And no matter how enthralling it might have been for the rest of the companions to follow this unresolved incident to some end, their attention was suddenly wrenched by the harsh and abrupt laughter. A laugh that burst forth and began to emanate from the forest, a cruel, gratingly mocking laugh drawing quickly closer and closer. Its dissonant echoes were still grating across their ears when, from out of the shadows, appearing against the curtain of blood red eyes, emerged the black horseman. And surrounding him, above his head and all around, swarmed the hideous imps. These little beasts, like grotesque miniature people twisted into the shape of bats, seemingly covered the sky above the forest, a dark moving mass blinking with the small fires that occasionally flared out from the almost infinite number of their momentarily silent mouths. Now, as the laugh of the dark rider slowly faded into the night with the imminence of his arrival, the company on the clearing could hear only the overwhelming whirring of their wings and feel only that indescribable chill cutting straight to their bones, setting the stage for the approaching black menace.

And what a terrifying sight the horseman was! While Žarko had felt fear even at their first encounter, it now seemed as if his heart was frozen. On this occasion there was nothing left for the light to reveal, nothing ridiculous to be seen. The night had shrouded the hint of blush on the rider's cheeks, straightened his disheveled hair, softened the tattered clothing – as if the night had been the missing element in their first encounter. Even his bloodshot eyes now had a flaming splendor, bearing no resemblance to the redness of tiredness or drunkenness, but possessing a clear, unbridled cruelty. Before the companions stood a figure of twisted royalty, haughty and callous, endlessly terrible in its sinister stance, which emanated from every part of the rider's body, every piece of his vestments, even from the horse on which he rode. And Žarko, for the first time, believed in some of Marena's words – that in front of them, poised, was indeed the true lord of the night, vampire or not!

The horseman had resumed his arrogant and hideous laughter as he rode slowly out of the forest, with this terrifying cackle acting almost as a servant, advancing ahead of the rider himself to pierce the very hearts of his opponents; and mercilessly it persisted, ringing out and echoing, finally ceasing only when the horse, having made a few slow steps, brought his rider completely out into the clearing. Then the dark rider spoke, his voice now completely free of all the hoarseness and rasping strain that Žarko remembered clearly from their first meeting. Now the speaker's voice was youthful and resonant like a crystal bell, reminiscent even of Miloš's, but possessing an unmistakable note of unshackled violent intent; one could not say whether the sound it made was pleasant or unpleasant to the ear, for the utterance of each word sent needles shivering up the skin of every listener.

"We meet again, mad Žarko… We meet, though for you it would be better that we do not! Did I not tell you plainly: 'Beware, Žarko, that your path does not lead you across mine again?' I see that you have not heeded me, so now you must reap what you have sown!"

Žarko did not want to waste this unexpected chance. Instead of answering, he suddenly and swiftly hurled his battle spear, aiming for the horseman's heart! It was a powerful throw, and the spear cut briskly through the night air, yet even more quickly the rider swung his enormous saber with astonishing agility, knocking the flying spear sideways and just off its intended mark. The bladed head of the diverted spear still managed to strike the armor of the breastplate, but it just glanced off its front and fell to the side, like a branch attacking a stone wall. What devil's armor was this, that not even Žarko's strongest throw could penetrate?! And the momentum itself, which would knock even the best warrior off his horse, was simply not enough against this adversary – after a slight twitch, he remained stoically seated on his horse, which, under the force of the blow, swayed to the side, but kept its footing, then gave a loud and menacing neigh of victory. The horseman glared furiously at Žarko's band of companions for a dire moment, and then screamed:

"Onward, horde: time for us to feed!"

And in shrieking his command, the face of the horseman seemed to visibly warp and stretch, like a mask tearing, losing with these final words any remote trace of raw beauty and humanity, and what remained in its stead was nothing but sheer, bared malice. The demon wolves rushed in from all open sides, running forward past the horseman in a furious charge towards the luckless bunch trapped atop the rise.

Even as the short speech of the horde's leader unfurled, the two Morlaks, as they called themselves, still pressed on in chanting at Vuk in almost hypnotic rhythm, so focused that they paid no attention whatsoever to the events closing in upon them:

"Remember yourself, lame wolf! You must remember – only your calling can summon us when it is not our time! Remember yourself, chieftain-Vuk, remember who you are or this night will take us all!"

Vuk looked as if snared in confused turmoil. His attention constantly shifted back and forth, from the entrancing babbling of the two barefoot figures, to the events unfolding on the edge of the forest. He visibly twitched, upset, when the wolves lunged forward on command. Žarko and Miloš, meanwhile, awaited the rush, well-prepared for battle: the saber cut through the air first, slicing down two of the animals in one swoop, the first's severed head flying off the remainder of its body, while the slashing motion continued through the other's open mouth, gaping the demonic jaws even wider; the return stroke then cut through the forelegs of the third monstrous attacking animal, leaving it snapping its terrible jaws in vain through the open air, while still furiously sliding on the ground just a few steps from its unbitten victim; yet another charging hellhound stumbled upon the wriggling fallen body, only to be met by the sharp point of Miloš's unrelenting curved blade. Meanwhile, with one mighty swing of his enormous battle mace, Žarko took down three of the demons at once, tossing them aside to the left like a bloodied furry mass, striking in their misshapen flight several more beasts who were racing up from the other side and disabling their progress. The now fevered cripple, despite his confusion, managed to raise the staff he had been given by Miloš and at the last moment strike one of the beasts that had somehow made it through, staggering it momentarily, while Brado, in the blink of an eye, jumped on its back, extinguishing it deftly with his knife before straightening back up, as if nothing had happened, and rejoining Vukan in their frantic incantation: "Remember, Vuk, remember, leader, remember for all of us, for our time is running out! Remember, chieftain-Vuk, remember who you are!"

Then, finally, Vuk remembered.

– Chapter 18 –
Eyes in the Dark

Marena, seemingly dismissed by the men from the onset, had been holding back beside the tree together with Senka as the battle ensued and intensified. Now though, determining that the moment had arrived for her to act, she stepped forward, leaving a safer place under the sheltering boughs, and raised her strange staff high into the air. Chanting out a series of cryptic verses of her own, not minding the men of Morlak, her voice seemed to double in force with each new phrase, as her invocation grew in pitch and volume until it climaxed in a shriek. At the height of this wail, she thrust her staff down with all of her force, driving the bottom end deep into the ground. Both red stones at its crown now glowed with a bright, saturated light, so intense that it hurt to look upon it, and the whole head of the witching staff flared up in a white translucent flame, above which rose a thick spiral of smoke. The smoke began to spread as it ascended, but not like the smoke of an ordinary fire, bending instead unnaturally forward, like an extending hand, grasping towards the sea of flying creatures perched over the forest. This witching smoke quickly reached the throng of imps, who in their unfathomable mass had already begun to descend upon the small rise, their licks of flame now intensified to the point of spurting constantly from their small vicious mouths.

Meanwhile, a lame man named Vuk… he remembered. In a staggering flash of recollection beyond words and prehension, his body suddenly began to convulse into the throes of a terrifying transformation, just as the white light of Marena's staff illuminated the round knoll upon which they stood, blinding everybody and halting, momentarily, the furious attack of their enemies. The cripple's arms began to stretch and thicken, bursting through the sleeves of his torn shirt. His chest broadened, tearing through the remainder of this shirt, which now hung like rags about his body. His thighs began to swell in size, stretching his wide pants to their limits, clearly displaying the absurd musculature of his transformed legs. The hair on his chest began to thicken and erupt in waves, so even the naked eye could see a fur-like mass crawling over him like an army of ants, enveloping his neck and muscles, finally covering his entire body. His nose and jaw began to elongate, becoming one, like the snout of a beast. Then he dropped forcefully to the ground on his knees and hunched over, still a man, but with his human cries becoming more and more animalistic in their nature. And when he finally rose again, rising up from the last shudders of his wakeful transformation, he was no longer a man, for his humanness was left only in traces. The upper half of his body was now almost completely wolf-like, the nails of his hands elongated, sharp, and curved into claws. Claws had also sprung out of his toes, breaking through his shoes, now tattered by this powerful metamorphosis, while his head had taken on the form of a monstrous animal. And he raised that beastly head of sharp teeth and pricked ears, ripping apart and off with one hand (if it could still be called a hand) the remnants of his ragged shirt, casting it upon the ground like a snake removing its shed skin. The fearful maw then turned towards the full moon above the forest and let out a long, drawn-out howl. A howl akin to those that had chased them all these past hours, but with something savagely primeval in it – it was the cry of an animal finally liberated, freed after being caged for too long, a cry that screamed out its painful freedom, heralding the beast to the world again and calling out its long-lost pack. And upon this call, the two men from Morlak dropped down to their knees and fell into spasms of their own transformations. But he, who now carried his name proudly, did not wait for them. No, this Vuk, this "Wolf" in full embodiment of its name, jumped straight into the devilish wolves, like a wolf among sheep, for – hark! – the paragon and primal alpha of the Morlaks had returned. The primordial werewolf chieftain was born again.

All the while, the glimmering light from Mara's staff was unleashing a wave of confusion upon the assailants. The demonic beasts paused, turning their heads from the light, and began to pull back to the darkness of the forest in a cacophony of shrill growls and pained yelps. The imps as well shrieked from the sudden unexpected light, but it was the smoke itself that made them retreat, the conjured smoke that had risen up as if guided, hounding them and dispersing across their multitude, which in fits of panic began to scatter apart in all directions. Even the black horseman himself flinched for a moment, letting out a scream of surprise while covering his eyes with his arm, but he just as quickly recovered, jumping from his frightened horse straight into the throng of retreating animals. Landing nimbly on his feet, he then ripped apart the air with a piercing cry: "Žaaarkooo! I will feast on your blood tonight!" And almost like Vuk, who was still in the throes of his own shapeshifting, the lord of the night now unveiled his true form, until then still masked in black robes and shadows: his face had completely distorted, his mouth opening into a gape twice as wide as it seemed possible, all his teeth protracting into long fang-like spikes, the nails on his hands extending sharply into sickles, seeming to wrap around the hilt of his giant sabre, while his eyeballs bulged forth as if torn out of their sockets just before he leapt at his prey with such speed that eyes could barely follow the movement.

Žarko and Miloš, just as their attackers, had also been startled by the sudden appearance of light that had abruptly illuminated their knoll, but Žarko braced himself for this assault in time, dodging the fierce attack of the dismounted horseman, while also swinging his mace to meet the oncoming blade. Several of the six sharp points of the mace-head grabbed the blade as if biting down on it, shattering it to pieces, and leaving the attacker with only a shank in his hand. The vampire, for this surely was a vampire, threw down the remainder of his sword, turning around on the spot and twisting with a supernatural elasticity, slamming his shoulder into Žarko who still sought to evade the attacker's lunge, all of this before the shattered pieces of the blade had met the ground. The warrior was knocked back from this blow, and as he fell backwards, he kept his eyes fixed on the two sharp unsheathing fangs that were rising with the attacker's gaping maw and rushing for his neck faster than he could fall. As he tumbled down, Žarko attempted to swing his mace again, but his enemy prevented the intended blow with a rapid grab of his hand, gripping hard onto Žarko's own and stopping him in the act (a feat beyond the power of any mortal man), forcing him to release the weapon. As if he had expected this, however, and completely in control of himself despite the danger, the warrior completed the motion of his left hand, which he had begun at the same time as his attempted swing of the mace with his right. This movement froze the horrific grin that had begun to form on the face of his assailant – the mustached man had imperceptibly pulled his knife from its belt-sheath, and, in an adder's flash, stabbed the blade between the loosely-hanging tails of the vampire's ringmail, directly into its lower stomach, then slashed violently upwards until the blade hit against the lower edge of the unbreakable breastplate.

Žarko rolled to the side quickly as the vampire tumbled to the ground, his hand gripping the handle of Žarko's knife. He groaned, bewilderingly gazing at the blade sticking out of him. But this glimmer of seeming dismay lasted but a fleeting moment, for he then looked up approvingly in Žarko's direction, like a hunter pleased with the vigor of his impending prize, while Žarko, with a shudder of horror, watched as his opponent straightened back up with ease, pulling the knife slowly out of himself. And now the groan transformed slowly into condescending laughter, as the hero and anti-hero held each other's eyes: "Žarko, you fool, that will not work here… try and come at me now, brute, when you are out of weapons!" And again he threw himself at Žarko, knocking him back to the ground just as he managed to stand up.

The large man struggled furiously to grab the vampire by the neck and somehow managed to pull the monster into a lock upon his chest. Knotted together thusly, Žarko squeezed and squeezed that neck with all his might, with the strength he was widely known for, but this devil just kept on laughing. He cackled, on and on, and yet he could not free himself. His hands scrambled savagely, trying to free up his head and teeth for a wound, but they could find no chance. In this embrace, the combatants struggled, rolling left and right upon the ground, each seeking to gain any advantage, yet neither would give in. Žarko felt fear, fear like he had never felt before, drawing on every last bit of dwindling strength left in him. But this was not enough – the longer this strained embrace lasted, the more it seemed as if the vampire would prevail; despite all his effort, the mustached man could not even move his back off the ground, let alone do something more.

It was just then, pinned to the ground with his hope and stamina waning, that Žarko noticed Miloš standing behind him and looking at him, keeping to the side of the scuffle and a ways off, so as not to be noticed. Their eyes met and again they understood each other without a word being spoken – Žarko feigned as if he was about to give in, releasing with his right hand the vampire's left, which immediately plunged its nails down, scratching deep into his cheek. The warrior groaned in pain, and, in what seemed like desperation, swayed to the side and pushed the vampire off him, yet in the same movement grabbed the handle of the sabre which Miloš had thrown through the air towards him, and, with uncanny deftness, finished the slashing action which had begun with an empty hand.

With this one powerful and precise stroke, the blade sliced through the descending vampire's neck, severing completely its head from the body! As the head rolled, with a terrible grimacing smile of triumph frozen on its face, Žarko straightened decisively, barely able to climb to his feet from exhaustion, and squeezed from his lungs one last rough shout at his fallen foe: "Laugh now, phantom head!"

Just then he heard a shout from behind: "The moth! Don't let the moth escape!" He turned around quickly towards the voice, not comprehending in his extreme fatigue what Mara's blathering about some moth could possibly mean, until he followed her gaze – from the mouth of the severed head, which had rolled off several steps away from the body, something was emerging. Žarko jumped quickly in that direction, but too late – already this moth, barely visible, pitch black like the night, had spread out its wings and rose up to the air. The man lunged forward and stretched out his hand in a final attempt to reach this black butterfly, but he missed, landing hard on his stomach and only bumping the severed head unintentionally, pushing it several steps further from the body. He scrambled up once again, but could now only stand, helplessly watching the nearly invisible black wings fading further and further into the night sky, and it seemed like he heard again, from somewhere far off, that familiar debased laughter hauntingly echoing on and on. The moth had escaped.

This entire battle with the vampire had transpired in

but a flash, before Vuk's transformation was even complete. As it had unfolded, the demon wolves had retreated to the forest, visible here and there and everywhere as they prowled amongst the trees, growling threateningly, their eyes still showing through the darkness in a bloody red glow. The light which had emanated from the top of Mara's staff had begun to dissipate, and the nightmarish pack appeared to be just waiting for it to extinguish entirely to launch into attack again. It was then that the werewolf went hunting, and it was then that Senka disappeared, her silent absence then still unnoticed.

– Chapter 19 –
The Snake King

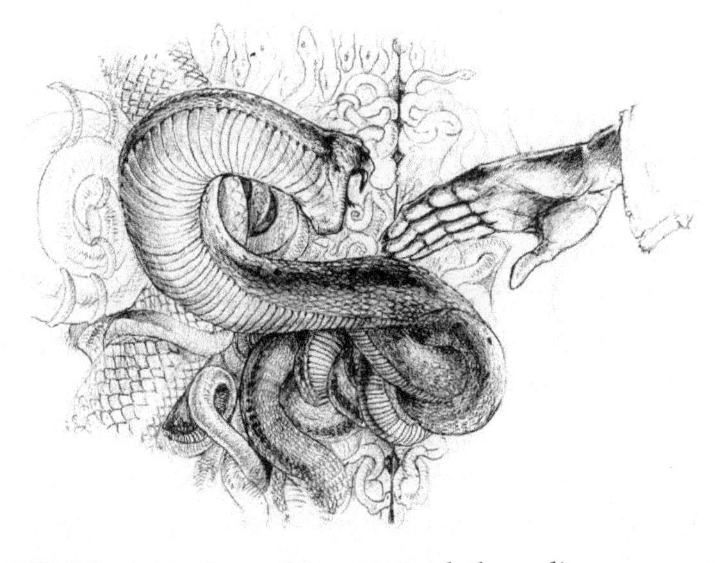

Before the others noticed her disappearance, Senka was already far away. When the sudden, supernatural light had emanated from Mara's staff, penetrating even the darkness of her unseeing eyes and causing her to blink in reaction, she had simultaneously heard that strange lisping voice, as if it were whispering directly into her ear, urging her up:

"Now... essscape... now... essscape..." And Senka immediately followed the voice's urging without a question, as if she had been waiting for it. She resolutely pulled Vidra up, then followed the dog as it led her off to the right side of the knoll, holding tight to the poisonous, thorny crop of bushes, and then straight into the forest, thronging with their enemies.

Surrendering to Vidra's instincts and the voice in her head, she somehow succeeded in making her way through the army of beasts, aided by the their temporary blinding at the unexpected and powerful light. Still, looking back later, she could not say just how she and her dog, with such sureness, managed to maneuver amongst the wolves and the trees, somehow passing hiddenly and silently through the perils surrounding them with nary an encounter. As if something much greater than they had set out a path for them, arranged so that they were always in the right place at the right time – stopping behind a tree trunk, downwind of a passing danger, or sheltered by dark cover, then moving again when opportune. They moved just as her name, Senka – shadow – would move, as noiseless as it was possible to be. She completely trusted this invisible guide, just as she trusted Vidra, whose fur she could feel constantly under her hand. While holding her breath as long as she could again and again, she felt not fear, but instead a restive excitement. She had taken her fate into her own hands (or at least believed this so), rather than wait helplessly for the uncertain end of a perilous battle. She expected that the others would fight fiercely for themselves, but in truth, she gave them little thought – so deeply was she wrapped in her own mind that it now seemed as if a blockade stood against any thoughts that might persuade her against this choice to venture into the unknown.

They had already moved quite a ways when Vidra suddenly shifted, causing Senka to fall to the ground. Her vacant eyes had no way of seeing the demon wolf with its blood red eyes racing violently yet voicelessly straight for them. Vidra though, without so much as a snarl, and not wavering even a second to bristle his fur, went staight at the beast, its bared fangs thirsty for blood. In falling, Senka only made out the vague sounds of a struggle, and one barely recognizable squeal, before the slamming of her own body against the forest floor was met by the thud of another body, slumping to its final gasps. For a moment after, all she could hear were the distant sounds of the battle behind them, and then she felt Vidra beside her, pushing at her arm with his head, urging her onwards once again. That which she had not seen, and which her ears had only captured in fragments and traces while her mind recoiled from the flurry, had all happened in the blink of an eye. A blink during which her dear dog, without warning or hesitation, charged at a wolf twice his size, turning into a seemingly no less terrible beast than the one silently coming their way. The attack was precise – the dog's jaws clamping onto the wolf's neck with a barely audible wrenching and then pulling backwards viciously, tearing away a large chunk of the wolf's neck in its mouth.

The creature gasped, trying to snap at the dog for the first and last time and failing, then crumpled to the ground at the same time as Senka; its legs were still kicking in the air as Senka raised herself up, leaning on Vidra's back. As they quietly stepped away, the pair of gleaming eyes watched on helplessly until their dimishing glow extinguished, returning the demon back to the hell from which it had sprung.

Step by step, the pauses of necessity became rarer and rarer. While not moving at a very fast pace, they were surely and steadily, if gradually, leaving the ever-quieter din of the battle far behind them. Until finally, and seemingly suddenly, all the traces and sounds which had been reaching them vaguely disappeared, completely lost to the silence of the forest night. This happened so abruptly that it felt as if they had simply stepped from one place into another, closing an imaginary door behind them. Senka heard one owl cry out nearby, and then felt a gentle wisp of air on her face, realizing that the creature was heading windward. They were safe, this she knew. Then again that rasping voice appeared right at her ear, so that the girl almost jumped. "Jussst a little bit more... go on..." And Senka continued forward.

After some dim, indefinite period of time, at last they arrived to the place that appeared to be their destination, for the voice rose and commanded more sharply: "Ssstop! Jussst a few more stepsss and we sstand before the gate. It will open willingly, for you have been sssummoned." The voice then seemed to swish loudly, or perhaps let out a strong hiss, and Senka made a few more steps before opening a gate – one leading to the realm of the snakes.

Again some intrinsic force overwhelmed all the doubts that might have whirred in her mind, impelling her onward, so she was neither vexed nor startled by the strange smoothness of the gate's handle, a handle which seemed to wind as if with its own will, pulling unnaturally under her hand. If she could have seen, it might have been harder for her to remain so calm, for the handle of this curious gate was a snake, alive or so true to life it would have been hard to say otherwise, whose head, open mouth, and forked tongue were turned upon the rest of its body, serving as the handle, exactly as if it were ready to bite down on any hand attempting to press it in hopes of opening the gate. And not just the handle, but the entirety of the two-winged gate, wider and taller than a man, with two doorposts crowned by snakes whose gazes mirrored back at one another, was made up entirely of snake bodies, interweaving into unimaginable ornaments that constantly writhed delicately, shifting in appearance before the eyes of any would-be entranced onlookers, yet somehow retaining structure and symmetry. This time, however, the only eyes taking in the spectacle were those of a dog, who showed no apparent alarm at such potential danger. And the dog's animal instincts were not mistaken, for the snake's mouth perched over the handle did not strike Senka's outstretched hand as the strange gate slowly opened, or so Senka envisioned, to the sounds of bodies slithering. In truth, the gate did not actually open; rather, the snakes simply twisted their bodies about, releasing the pressure on the handle, and opened into a window of passage large enough for them to pass through. And thusly a blind girl and her dog stepped though into a place where no man or dog had long set foot, if ever.

Once they had passed through the gate, the snake bodies that composed its breadth again wound back into living ornaments, closing the passage behind the visitors just as they had opened it. Leaving the gate behind them, the guests slowly advanced along a narrow path surrounded on all sides by tall, arching poisonous briars – the exact same sort which grew on the knoll where the battle they had abandoned had finished moments before. While on this path, the voice finally revealed to Senka the purpose of their visit here. Its manner of speaking remained hoarse and faltering, but Senka had little trouble making out its words: "Do not fear, even though you are now being led into the serpent kingdom. The Snake King is my father. When we come to his court, since you saved me from the fire, he will offer you whatever you wish: silver, gold, precious stones. But do not accept any of these, and seek only the gift of primal language! He will resist at first, but, in the end, he will give in, even if only after you have refused everything offered and have turned to leave with no reward at all."

And with this they arrived at the foot of the snake king's lair, pulling the girl back from the swirl of her thoughts. Hissing suddenly erupted from all sides, and for a moment Senka was frightened, abruptly aware that all around her were snakes. Her dog, remarkably, remained once again completely calm, not even the hair of his coat rising as it would in response to perceived danger, and this settled the girl to some degree. Then she heard the strange voice at her ear one last time: "Ssstay now, sssister, I mussst sssay farewell..." And the peculiar coldness that she had felt around her neck, for so long now that she had become accustomed to it, at once released, her necklace once again taking the form of a living snake, which gracefully unwound from about her neck and slipped down her arm, then descended gently onto the floor of the snake palace. (Senka thought for a moment, with a scarce hope, that perhaps her sight might also return, but it did not.)

Then once more she heard, from a short distance, a hissing in whose traces she could recognize that familiar voice which had long dwelt so closely to her ears, yet now alongside it was a much more powerful hiss, which seemed to be responding to it. Following this brief exchange, Senka found herself in the imposing presence of the snake king! The serpent was colossal, a snake so immense it could hardly be thought to exist, yet to Senka it seemed, from the nature of his voice, that he could be mistaken for a wise old man, for the snake spoke to her in a voice entirely human in its quality, which, unlike the one she had come to know at her ear, was completely free of any sort of rasping or faltering; as clean and clear as the voice of a man.

"What do you wish for me to give you for saving my

son?" he asked straightforwardly. Senka was confused for a moment, but then remembered her instructions and answered: "I want nothing but the gift of primal language!" To this the snake king replied: "That is not for you, young one, for if I were to indeed give you this, and you were to tell anyone of your gift, you would die immediately. Instead, tell me what else you are wishing for, whatever it is, and I will gladly grant it to you."

– Chapter 20 –
The Hunters and the Hunted

The warrior and the shepherd who fought as one were momentarily shocked and even a bit petrified, when just after their moment of seeming victory over the fallen horseman another monstrous beast rushed past them on all fours, brushing Žarko just slightly as he passed so that the heavy warrior spun around once again from the might of this accidental touch. It was hard to recognize Vuk, or that which had become of him, as the two men had been so fully occupied during his metamorphosis, that they could hardly guess at what this new marvel might be that now charged furiously into their attackers. Nor did they manage to get a good view of him now, for Vuk, in the blink of a mortal eye, had already plunged into the forest – the hunters, abruptly, had become the hunted.

The imps, in the mean time, had scattered on all sides, fleeing before the strange smoke still clutching after them. Their cries were already becoming lost in the distance, taking with them also some of that unnatural chill that always seemed to accompany them.

The forest, meanwhile, began to resonate with a strange commotion. At first, only a few wild growls could be heard, but these were almost immediately followed by a horrible din of squealing and shrieking as the wrenched bodies of the hellish wolves were tossed into the air left and right above the forest, like ragdolls thrown around in the tantrum of an angry child, branches breaking and the crowns of trees tearing from the force of their shattered flight. Then two more of these wolfish-human monsters rushed past the stunned eyes of the companions, dashing across the clearing and into the forest, which seemed to have come alive. Above it, every few moments, flew the remnants of what had been terrifying red-eyed wolves, who could now muster no shred of resistance in the face of these much more terrible hunters. From out of the forest, the body of one of these wolves flew upon the clearing, slamming into the ground just in front of Žarko and Miloš, who barely managed to avoid being hit. Withdrawing a few steps backward, they marveled in observing what had become of the beast: off of its neck had been torn a chunk of flesh larger than a man's outstretched fist, as if it had been ripped off in one voracious bite, while one leg hung off, attached only by a meager scrap of the animal's hide, which had been shredded by claws as if chopped brutally by an axe. Žarko looked at Miloš, who returned his astonished stare: "Well, it is good, brother, that we are not to also fight with these!" exclaimed the befuddled large man, and with that both of them broke into a laugh full of relief. The battle, at least for them, looked as though it was finished, and they found themselves not only alive, but also the unexpected victors!

✡✡✡

The demon wolf bodies were still bursting here and there above the forest when the warrior turned to survey the area around him. Vuk was not there, nor Vukan or Brado, but it was now clear to all where they had gone. Marena was standing listlessly, her eyes closed, leaning wearily on her peculiar staff – it looked as if she was completely spent from the spell she had conjured for their party, and Žarko thought with wonder for a moment at how perhaps it was her contribution to their victory that had proved decisive. But just then, suddenly, he realized that there was no Senka!

A deep fright instantly seized his heart, a fear he seldom felt. He began to look quickly about, to see if she was hiding somewhere on the knoll, that strange battlefield of their unexpected victory. He called out her name several times without a response, then asked Miloš if he knew where she was, at which both of them began briskly moving through and about the dark shadows of the trees bordering the rise, searching for any trace of the young girl. Near one tree along the outer rim, Miloš soon came across the hunting dagger which he had placed in her hand. Even Mara opened her eyes for an instant, following their tracking, only to immediately drop her head back down tiredly, resuming her seeming meditation.

A good deal of time was passed in this unsuccessful search, the warriors so focused that they failed to notice the gradual calming of the tussle in the forest until they finally returned, confused and anxious, to the tree at the center of the small hill. Other than the knife, there was no trace of Senka to be found! It was at this point that Vuk emerged from the trees. He was again in his human form, leading behind him the horse who until recently had been ridden by the vampire, with Brado and Vukan following one stride back. And while the two of them looked more or less as they had before, their scarce clothing perfectly adapted to that shapeshifting, Vuk was quite a comic sight as he advanced in tattered remnants of garments, his clothes hanging like bits of rags on all sides. That is, it would have been comic had Žarko been in a less troubled mood. Vuk had called out from the edge of the forest as they emerged, perhaps wishing to ensure them of their still friendly intentions: "It is over, master Žarko. Those we did not kill have retreated. And we killed many – all of the Morlak men are here, guarding the approach. They fought alongside me. Morlaks, my tribe... they had been following us from a distance, and came running at my call, attacking beasts everywhere. Very few escaped – the forest is covered in carcasses. There will be plenty of new vests..." And with this Vuk smiled, though he remained standing a bit off, as if waiting for permission to approach.

Žarko looked at him and nodded, trying to listen, but his thoughts were still occupied with Senka's whereabouts. "You have much to tell us, my friend and fellow Vuk, for from this night you are no longer my servant, but a brave companion in the thick of our troubles... but that story will have to wait, for trouble, it seems, has not..." And Žarko went on to tell them quickly of Senka's disappearance; Vuk confirmed that they had not seen her in the woods, with Vukan and Brado silently nodding their heads in agreement. Despite the rightful tiredness they all felt, having only just finished the battle, they began devising a plan straight away on how to split up and search for the girl, when, in the middle of their conversation, Mara interrupted sharply. She raised her head, opening her eyes only with apparent difficulty, but in a clear voice proclaimed, slightly mockingly, in the way only she could: "Do not waste your time foolishly – no one can find Senka, she cannot be found!"

At this, Žarko erupted. He forgot in a flash Mara's pivotal role in all that had unfolded that night, and angrily jumped at her, grabbing her by both arms, so that she dropped the staff on which she had been leaning, then started shaking her like some toy rattle: "Where is Senka, witch's daughter?! Speak, or you will cease to be!"

"I do not know, Žarko… I do not know! Much still remains hidden from me!"

Žarko lessened his grip and let off his shaking of the young woman, so she continued: "Most importantly, what I do know is this: she no longer is in our reach. Our night's trials have finished, but Senka is yet to face her own. Still, if all goes well, she will return to us, and will do so before dawn. But until then, we cannot do anything for her. Ours is but to wait, and we should do that right here where we are."

The strange young woman then again dropped off into silence, finally allowing herself to close the eyes she had barely kept open. Žarko looked at her, continuing to hold her up, as if he was thinking over whether to shake her again, but Miloš approached, putting a hand on his shoulder. "Let us leave off mad inquiry, Žarko. You cannot have forgotten already how the witch has helped us? She has not yet given us reason not to trust her, perhaps we should listen…"

And thus, word by word and relenting nod, the men assented not to head out on a search that night, but to wait for morning, and head out at first light, if Senka did not appear by then. All of them were beyond tired and nearly all wounded, so it was agreed that for the remainder of the night they would camp on the knoll, and that their search for Senka would begin as soon as there was enough light for their eyes to be of help. Vuk, who in his recent other form was unhampered by night, declared them secure where they were, with no need for watch shifts, for the Morlak men were on the lookout deep into the woods. Vukan and Brado announced that they would go in search of some herbs that would ease the pain of their wounds and help heal them as well, while Vuk offered to hunt some meat "much better than wolf" for their dinner. And saying so, he stepped forward towards Žarko with the reins of the horse, which he had been holding the entire time they had talked.

"This steed needs a master, one far better than its previous one." But Žarko shook his head, saying that such a horse would do far better under Miloš, rather than slave until death under him. And so Miloš accepted the reins of the kingly horse, who now seemed tame and calm. From its demeanor, it was apparent that the horse had been well-trained, and Miloš wondered to himself how such a stallion had come into hands of its former master. As he thought over this, he led the horse over to where their other stood, also calm now, and tied them together, then set about gathering some branches for a campfire, while Vuk went off after his prey, dissolving into the forest dark. Out of the corner of his eye, Miloš thought he caught a glimpse of Vuk changing into his other form in midstep, but when he raised his head to look in that direction, the figure had already disappeared from sight and into the woods.

Before even half an hour had passed, a large fire was already blazing on the modest hill to roast the large wild goat which Vuk had brought back from his hunt. Returning in his human form, it seemed as if he was struggling, lame as he was, to haul the great animal, so Miloš stepped forward to help him. Vukan and Brado then rubbed the herbs they had meanwhile gathered into everyone's wounds, starting with Vuk, then moving onto themselves, and lastly assisting the rest of the companions. Žarko marveled at the pleasant feeling these herbs immediately brought about, driving off the pain of the deep scratches made by the vampire's claws.

Later, as they ate sitting around the fire, Žarko and Miloš finally got around to asking Vuk about his role in this night's events, to which he replied simply, yet evasively: "Some things are too difficult to capture in words, so please, don't press me to try, for I would not be able to tell." Žarko appeared disappointed by such a response, frowning so that his whiskers stretched out, but Miloš only shrugged his shoulders and turned the conversation in another direction, launching into a convincing account of how the battle was brought to its victorious end. In his narration, he talked up the contributions of every member of the party, while downplaying his own. And, as he had expected, the other men gladly accepted this magnanimous version of events, drinking in the still sweet taste of victory, and talking happily away into the night longer than they had expected. The jovial atmosphere overcame even the somewhat chilling feeling given off by Mara, who stood off to the side, still silent and with closed eyes, yet ever leaning weakly on her peculiar staff, which she had picked up from the ground after being released by Žarko.

If it were not for Senka's disappearance, it would have been a truly pleasant night, and a joyful celebration of a hard-won victory.

– Chapter 21 –
The Gift of Primal Language

The snake king was waiting for her reply. "So, then, what do you wish from me? Would you like such a large pile of silver, that you could live easily for the rest of your life?" The blind girl refused the offer firmly – not only had she been told to do so by the smaller snake that made her blind, but she truly did not long for wealth. "Would you prefer gold then, if silver does not suffice? So much gold that you and your children would live easy for your entire lives?" Senka again resolutely refused, repeating that her only desire was the gift of primal language. "That is not for you, I told you! Would you not rather be given precious stones from the depths of the earth, the likes of which human eyes have never seen? You, your children, and their children would have no worries for wealth through all of your days!" To this Senka answered firmly once again, even if inside a piece of her could not help but be drawn by the thought of such extravagant wealth: "If you would like to bestow a gift upon me, give to me the gift of primal language. And if you cannot, then gods be with you and farewell. I do not need anything else." And in saying this, Senka indeed pulled at Vidra, turning about in her place as if to leave, and slowly began withdrawing in the direction from which they had come.

Only then did the snake king relent, calling her to return with his words: "Wait! Walk over here, if this is truly what you want... your ancestors souls amongst us whisper that you might be ready. And indeed you have earned it: you have lost one kind of sight, so you may now receive this other. Come." At this, Senka slowly approached the voice, thinking over the words about her ancestors, but not understanding what the king had said. "Open up your mouth!" commanded the snake king. Senka did so, and the snake king spit on her tongue! She did not immediately realize what had happened, only feeling an unfamiliar taste in her mouth, until the snake king commanded her next: "Now you spit into my mouth." And what else could she do but follow his demand, so she gathered a pinch of saliva in her mouth and spit it back, recognizing it was not the time to be unsettled despite the uneasy cramping that she suddenly felt in her stomach, and hoping that the king was positioned in front of her so that she would not errantly miss. Then the snake king again told her to open her mouth anew, and in this way three times they spit into each other's mouths, before the great serpent pronounced at last in his sage voice, like that of a venerable man:

"Now, young one, you have the gift of primal language. Along with this, I give you this reed pipe – it is to be used only once, when you are in the greatest of need; play each of its tones in order, from the highest to the lowest, and all the snakes around and near you will come to your aid as if you were the snake king himself! Now, depart, and farewell, but for your own sake, tell no one of your new ability, for if you speak of it, you will die on the spot!" And somehow the reed pipe appeared in Senka's free hand, which she quickly placed inside the clasps of her clothes, paying it little attention, for she was now abruptly focused fully on how to get out of this lair of snakes, suddenly bursting over with the gossiping voices of countless fork-tongued mouths speaking. Speaking! Senka, in a moment of sudden revelation, realized that she now understood these voices prattling in masses, whispering back and forth about her, asking and wondering how she had dared to come into their most sacred den, and to seek no less than the gift of primal language itself!

Completely overwhelmed and under the impression of her extraordinary realization, Senka simply let Vidra guide her, and the dog led her back to the gate without a misstep. Approaching the gate again, Senka now heard a sea of inquisitive voices, exclaiming their amazement that she carried no treasure with her. And the snakes whose bodies formed the gate pulled apart of their own accord, without any touch from Senka, making a passage for the girl and her dog, who stepped out of the serpent's kingdom and back into the forest followed by a multitude of goodbyes. The snakes were bidding her farewell, and Senka could understand them!

As they made their way back through the forest, Senka, slowly, began to grasp the full scope of the gift of this language she had received. It was almost as if she had her sight returned: everything that was alive before them spoke out in some way, unveiling her surroundings to her. The herbs whispered to her of the medicines they carried against ills, the trees offered their trunks for her to lean against and rest, to pick their fruits and spread their seeds to the far ends of the earth… that same owl still called out forlornly from the sea of branches, but Senka now understood her aching search for love in the night; in a state of near disbelief, Senka realized that she was even aware of every insect around them! None of these beings spoke in words like the snake king, nor resembled some human language, yet she simply somehow understood. It was not an intelligent, articulate speech all around her, but Senka could garner all kinds of knowledge from out of this murmur, and even more so exactly those bits which were of interest to her. The primal language… she began to understand what this was, and why it was truly primordial.

Unconsciously at first, surprising herself, Senka removed her hand from Vidra's back and, slowing her steps, continued to walk forward, now on her own. From all the primal voices which she could recognize with her new capability, she knew what was in front of her, as well what was to the side of her, below her, above her, and even behind. "It is like the old game of blind grandmother… where you walk with a blindfold through a sea of people who are playing around you and then they call out to you as you approach," she thought to herself, yet she could clearly hear each sound pouring forth from this sea of voices. And soon she realized that she could even focus this new gift of hers – like looking into the distance, making out what was further off, and suddenly instead of picking up on just the few trunks in front of her, she could feel a forest. Then her attention was drawn to Vidra, and in complete astonishment, she realized she now could even understand the "thoughts" of her pet! Or perhaps it would be better to say that she felt this, as the dog seemed concerned by her letting go, and very tensely stepped along in stride with her, expecting her at any moment to stumble and need the dog's help. And Senka suddenly let out a laugh, without any fear, for she "saw" all that was about her, and there was nothing in sight to be fearful of. She crouched down next to Vidra and gave him a robust hug, then straightened up again. "This is beautiful," she thought, and quickened her steps. Focusing again on the forest around her, she walked with more and more surety, knowing exactly what was before her – where a branch hung and at what height, and thus how much she would need to bend to avoid it. "This is better than sight," the thought raced through her head, as she realized that though completely blind, she could now move through the darkness like an owl, much more securely than she ever could have while she had been able to see!

Enchanted by the beauty of her newfound "sight," as the snake king himself had called it, Senka walked on unconscious of the time, focused only on the way, and thus it completely escaped her attention that the behavior of her dog had changed; just like with one's eyes, it was possible to look in the wrong direction with this new form of sight. The warning from her dog finally broke through her trance, as she became conscious of the immediate surroundings only with a considerable delay, somehow at the same time as she stumbled and fell flat to the ground, her whole length now against the forest floor.

Completely confused, she felt Vidra's muzzle at her neck, and with this she pushed herself up into a sitting position and reached her hands back, aiming for what had been the blank spot in her new form of vision, something which had seemed to say nothing and yet had somehow caused her fall. Her hand felt over a rough, crude type of fur, which was here and there covered in a thick, congealing fluid-like substance… blood! She twitched her arm backward, frightened, but then settled herself, willing herself to continue on again. As she explored further with her fingers, cautiously, fighting disgust, everything slowly became clear – she had tripped upon and was now perched over a dead animal. The primal language, she remembered, could only be voiced by the living. At the same time, she realized that this dead animal that she was touching was neither small nor harmless – the size of the teeth which she felt under her searching fingers sent shivers through her body as she determined decidedly that this creature had not died of any natural cause. Under her outstretched hand, at a place where she should have found the dead neck, she felt only a hole and a trickling mass of blood! Chilled and terrified, she anxiously pushed herself away from the corpse, wiping her hand through the grassy earth. Then she stood back up, grasping back onto Vidra's fur again for guidance, and they warily moved forward.

It was then that she finally remembered the battle, in the thick of which she had left so cowardly… but what could she have done, blind and helpless as she was? At least this way she was not a burden to the rest of the companionship, and could it have been that perhaps the attackers had called off their attack, whose goal had seemingly been to get her, and only her, for reasons unknown? Fear struck her suddenly… what if their enemies were now out here looking for her? But she quickly calmed, knowing that now she would feel such animals. Then again she felt a rush of fear, this time more stark: what about a vampire?! Would she be able to sense the undead? He could move with or without his animals... bewildered, she froze in her place. What could she – what should she – do? As had become her custom in the turbulence of these recent days, she once again resorted to staking her fate on the instincts of Vidra. The dog wanted to move on, and confidently at that; this was clear to Senka (even without her companion showing its inclination by any movement or action) and so she acquiesced, letting Vidra lead them wherever it desired.

They passed through the guard of the Morlak men; Senka had not been conscious of this, so she could not have begun to ask how, yet she had been seen and let pass through without a sound being made. It was not long after this that she heard voices. Human voices. And with a sense of relief akin to a stone being lifted from her heart, she recognized these voices as familiar. "... And then through these riddles of greeting I could make out this: 'a shepherd for wolves.' That one was a good one, Mara!" Miloš! And then the girlish voice answering him indistinctly, still unyielding despite its tiredness that weighted the laughter. But Miloš only went on more loudly, and now playing at strictness, which could not hide its mirth: "And now you tell me, Vukan and Brado: who are these stray wolves who grab our sheep right under the noses of my shepherds and dogs?!" This was greeted with a raucous laughter from the company... Vuk... and those strange men... and now again Mara!

They were alive!

And at this moment, Senka realized one more thing – that whenever a person would speak, she could "see" nothing but that person. The others would remain hidden from her. All but Žarko… his snoring broke through the voices of everyone else, refusing to be overpowered by even the uproar of their shared laughter, and seemed to be intensifying just then as Žarko tossed about in his dreams. And so, there it was, another limitation in her new powerful but not all-seeing gift – people do not speak primally, but only in the languages of man. Still, at this moment, it was not important, for her heart was bursting, beating faster and faster as she approached her companions. Both she and Vidra let their steps fly faster and faster, joyfully eager to find themselves back amongst the company of their friends.

– Chapter 22 –
Time for a Tale

Little sleep was had by the companions during this night, with the exception of Žarko. It is not hard to picture with what staggered relief the group, huddled about the dying fire on the knoll, greeted their missing companions. Vuk was the first to see her. "Senka!" he cried out, his voice clearly conveying the fullness of his honest joy as he clumsily scampered over to embrace her warmly. He then offered her his hand and led her to the fire, where the rest of the company waited eagerly, observing her with interest as well. Senka was aware of this, even if she could not see them, for her arrival had brought an abrupt end to their talks, and the stillness of the late night was for a brief moment only interrupted by the crackling of the wood on the fire and the sounds of Žarko's ceaseless tossing about in his dreams. While Vuk was helping the young girl sit down, Senka felt in her hand the tatters of what had been his garments and asked herself what all had happened in her absence. Miloš addressed her first, with a voice somewhat more brash than what she had grown accustomed to from him: "I am very glad to see you alive, little one. It seems as if Mara was right when she foretold that you would return on your own… Perhaps now you could tell us where you went off to?"

And so, for the first time, Senka was forced to deceive her friends. If it had already been hard for her previously to refrain from mentioning the recurring reappearance of the snake and its voice whispering in her ears, then her evasiveness now was truly agonizing – she could feel herself blushing from the pressure of these emotions, and hoped that the flickering firelight hid and masked this from their view. And she lied, for what else was there for her? If you were to tell anyone of your gift of primal language, you would die immediately! These dire words of the snake king echoed in her ears. She said that she had been frightened, and so she went off with Vidra, following the dog's lead in an attempt to escape, though how they actually managed to do so was beyond her. They went who knows how far, the dog leading the way throughout, eventually laying down on the forest floor under the protection of a tree, where they remained in silence for what seemed like a very long time. At last, the dog indicated a desire to return, and since Vidra appeared to sense that the danger had passed, they turned about and headed back… The story was not very convincing, even to her, and the doubtful murmurings of the others let her know clearly that they had not been entirely persuaded either. Still, no one pressed her further.

Little by little, the conversation picked up again and she was told that they had won the battle and that there was no longer any of the enemy about to pursue them, for whatever reason they had been hunting them until now. And with this, more for themselves than for her sake, the victors again launched into their accounts of the unusual course of the skirmish, once more basking in the glowing joy of victory. Mara brought Senka pieces of the roast meat, using the opportunity to whisper: "I see that you lost your necklace during your flight. It must have become tangled on some branch – surely, that is the source of this scratch on your cheek?" Senka did not hesitate in agreeing, then returned her attention to the meat, trying to create the impression that she was famished from hunger, just so as to avoid further questions. But for now, Mara did not speak even a word more, and Senka found herself wondering if perhaps she knew more than what she had said? Had this truly been a question, or maybe a subtle way of hinting at what she could say if someone else were to ask the same?

All this time, Miloš had been curiously studying, for who knows what time, the saber which he had received from Žarko, turning it about to examine it from all angles. "A remarkable blade, and a curious ornament," he mumbled, focusing on some unusual seal set between the three golden orbs decorated in precious stones on the hilt. This drew the attention of the others, who all stopped to regard the unique symbol, most particularly Vuk – in his eyes a spark of unusual curiosity flared, a kindling perchance of recognition: "Perhaps, Miloš, perhaps I can tell you of how Žarko came to be the wielder of this blade, for it seems to me unlikely that there is any other quite like it."

Miloš raised his head in wonder, asking how was it that Vuk could know something like that? Maybe Žarko had told him the story? Vuk only laughed, and then began to tell his tale:

"You already know well, Miloš, what kind of man is our Žarko: not much of a talker himself, but a creator of tales nonetheless, for about him and his feats, tales are spun and spoken in every corner of the world where this healthy leg has ever taken me to. One of these stories, which I heard a long time ago, perhaps tells exactly the tale of how Žarko garnered that blade, and likely as well the dagger, which, as you told us, he pulled out tonight. You heard that he calls this knife his 'secret adder,' and as for the sword, he spoke of having received it from a king that he did not serve, which to me suggests, along with the seal on the scabbard, that this story which I heard so long ago may indeed be the truth… so, to begin at the beginning…"

"It is told that all of this transpired immediately after the present king of the Hurs, having killed off his predecessor, claimed the throne. The Hurs were then not so powerful, nor as notorious as they are today. Perhaps you know, or perhaps not, that the current king does not have royal blood in his veins; in truth, he is not even a Hur by ancestry. However, he had for a long time surrounded himself with a dangerous group of warmongers in developing his plans to take forcefully the throne to which he had no claim by law – and while these were the kind of people he needed to come to power, they very soon became the chief source of trouble that threatened the stability and expansion of his reign. One of these men, his then right-hand man, was a particularly infamous barbarian, whose origins were unknown for it is said that he was black as the darkest night. This black warrior found far greater comfort in war than in peace, and it is he who stands as the principal warrior of this story."

Seeing that he had gained Miloš's full attention, Vuk continued with ease, beginning to revel even himself in his words: "All of this, then, began when this brute, spending the gold he had amassed under his former general and now his king, built for himself an enormous, towering castle by the sea. It is said that this castle was so luxurious that its like could be found nowhere else in the world, as if the warrior himself was trying to outdo the imperial court itself. After the building was complete, the tower windows decorated with the finest glass, and the floors draped in silk and velvet, the scoundrel sent a letter to his king whose contents were not exactly gracious...

Lord king: by the sea I have built a tower so great, but I have no one to walk its chambers with. As I have not yet married, give me your daughter as my lover. And if you choose not to – prepare yourself for another struggle.

This letter arrived to the new king, and he immediately realized the danger in which he now found himself – he did not know who amongst his rakish band of militants was loyal to him, and who to the barbarian, his second-in-command. If the king refused to give the girl to him, his dear daughter from his first wife, there would be trouble; but if he were to yield and indeed hand her over, the trouble would also inevitably arrive, just sometime later – especially since if he were to marry into royalty, the unscrupulous barbarian might have a legitimate path to the throne. For a son born from such a marriage would be the heir if the king himself did not produce a male child, meaning that the daring warrior, with this son as impetus, could attempt to take the throne by force.

So the king decided to find himself a hero and offered countless treasures to he who would defeat the barbarian. Many warriors answered the call, enticed by the rich rewards declared, but not one came back to Leđan – all of them were vanquished by the barbarian. The king was soon out of would-be champions to call on, and rather than the trouble being brought to an end, it was now more dire than ever: the black barbarian was preparing his move. He was readying himself in his white tower, donning himself in his knightly attire, girded with his curved saber and iron chain armor, while his silver mare was prepared; it was bridled with a golden bridle, his heavy war mace clasped to her flanks, and once adorned thusly, he finally swung up onto the horse's back, his battle spear readied at his side, and spurred off quickly from his sea palace, heading straight for Leđan. Accompanying him were twenty of his most trusted knights, horsemen who down to the last man would give their life for him – either out of love or out of fear that if they did not, they would face something far more terrible.

When he arrived at the gates of Leđan, he threw his spear into the ground, tying his horse to its shaft, unfurled and set down a huge tent, and then issued his demands to the city: every night a fat sheep must be delivered to the tent, as much bread as the party desired, one barrel of strong aged brandy, two barrels of fine red wine, and one beauty of a girl to serve the wine and brandy, while throughout the night he gets the pleasure of kissing her pretty white face.

In addition, he began to take tribute from anyone entering or exiting the city; in just three months, he amassed uncountable riches from this hoarding, while the royal coffers grew emptier and emptier. It was shameful for the king, shameful for the city. As it became clear to the king that this trouble would not resolve itself, he called upon all of his former bandits to rise against the barbarian at the city's gates! But, alas, no one wished or dared. And as no one else was willing to confront the barbarian on behalf of the king, neither was the king himself.

Nor was this the end of the troubles, for after three months the barbarian grew weary of waiting and drunkenly went riding through the city, finally heading for the king's castle. Upon reaching the gates, he shook them furiously, then stood back and roared out as loudly as he could: "You lazy king! Send out the girl!" He then unleashed his heavy mace, striking at the castle's gates, while his militant band of supporters broke whatever they could around them, then threw the rubble through the castle's windows, breaking the glass. The king now saw that the trouble had come all the way to his door, but he did not want to send his guard out to their deaths – instead, as he had already suffered a great deal of shame, he ruefully capitulated and swallowed some more: he shouted out from his tower, calling to the barbarian, asking him when he would like to come for the girl.

The boor gladly answered: "In 15 days, once I return from the coast with my decorated wedding party," then turned his mare around and rode away. But the king's daughter, who had overheard the exchange, shrieked out like an angry snake: "Oh my god, woe to me, the maiden! Why has this face been cared for, if it is to be given over to kiss the barbarian and let him do what he wants!" But the King gave his consent nonetheless, while the queen said nothing, making no entreaties to the king to change his mind (the queen was herself only a girl slightly older than the bride-to-be, and this was not her daughter at stake). And so the poor king's daughter now clearly saw the stark fate that awaited her.

That night, as the distraught maiden slept, it is said that a man spoke to her in her dreams, saying: "There is, my lady, a city of Prilip in a neighboring kingdom, and in that city is a hero of renown. Send a letter to this Žarko, begging for his brotherly help before the gods and promise to him boundless riches if he delivers you from the barbarian." And as soon as the girl awoke in the morning, she ran to her father, the lord king, to tell him of what she had dreamt. After listening to her account, the king urgently sent out a royal letter to this Žarko:

My son before God, hero Žarko! Come to my aid in my Leđan and defeat the blackest barbarian so that he does not take my daughter from me, and I will give thee three wagons of treasure!

The king's messenger had already been sent forth carrying the letter when the maiden remembered that in her dream she had been told to write to Žarko herself and began to worry that perhaps Žarko would not answer the king's entreaty. At this desperate thought, she jumped up, grabbing a feather and a scroll. With the sharp end of the feather, she stabbed her own face, and from her cheek blood began to trickle, a thick line of blood, and using it as her ink, or so they say," continued Vuk without pausing, "she wrote out her own plea which read:

My dear Žarko, brother under God's sky! I bless you before the God in heaven, and implore you before the god of Justice, and before your Dajbog the fiery! Do not let me be handed over to the blackest barbarian; I will give you six wagons of treasure, and as well offer a golden dagger: its handle is a coiled asp, like alive, in whose fangs are set precious stones, by whose emanating light you can see in darkness as in the day! And I will bestow unto you a sabre with three hilts of gold, inlaid with three precious gems, a blade worth more than three kingly cities; and I will emblazon it with the seal of king, so that under no condition can you be slain, even by a vizier, without the king being asked first!

And so she sent off her messenger to ferry her own letter to Žarko.

When the first messenger made it to Žarko, he read the letter inside, and then replied to the king's courier in the following words: "Go with greetings, king's letterman, bring them to my self-proclaimed forefather: I cannot fight this black barbarian; he is a masterful swordsman, a warrior of great fame, and he would slice my head from my shoulders. And with no head, what good to me would three wagons of treasure be?" The messenger urgently returned back to the king to deliver this message, when upon his leaving, the second courier arrived. Žarko was puzzled by this succession of events, but read through the second letter as well, then thought over the matter long and well, before calling the courier before him to hear his words of reply: "I am sorry, my sister before gods, that this evil has come to you – even worse cannot be!" not saying in the end whether he would indeed come, or would he not.

"When the second messenger departed, Žarko climbed up to the top of the tower where he was residing. He dressed himself for action, throwing his wolf cloak across his shoulders and pulling on the cap with the wolf's head; he clasped on his sword and scabbard, taking as well his battle spear, and then went down to the stables, where he filled one large wineskin full of red wine, which he hung on the horse's right side, while setting his battle mace on its left flank to balance things, so the animal would not totter to and fro. And with this, he hopped up in the saddle and quickly galloped off for Leđan, in a hurry to get there before this feared blackest of warriors."

Here, Vuk made a small pause and smiled knowingly, smug in his story being well received, then continued: "And when he arrived there…

Žarko did not go straight to the king, nor to any official, but rather directly to the city tavern. Here, at the inn, he arranged a stay for himself. After he freshened up, as dusk was approaching, he led his horse to the nearby lake to also drink and refresh itself from the cold water. But the horse refused to drink, and only turned about itself in protest. At this, Žarko also turned around, espying a young Hur girl, covered in a shawl, advancing straight toward the lake, having seen neither Žarko nor the horse.

As she approached its shore, she bowed to the lake, then spoke: "With my god as witness, green lake, you will be my eternal home! I will rather be joined with you than enter a union with the barbarian!" At hearing this, Žarko called out from the dark: "Good lady, what drives you into the lake? What terrible trouble?" The girl regarded him with surprise, dressed oddly as he was in his wolf's cap, then spoke: "Come now, poor dervish! Why do you ask when you can offer no help?" Nonetheless, in her desperate state, she went to tell him everything: that she was the king's daughter, and from what she was escaping by abandoning herself to the lake, ending with these words: "In my dream, I was told that in the city of Prilip, there was a hero by the name of Žarko, who could defeat the barbarian. I sent him my blessing from the Father of all gods in heaven, and blessed him before the god of Justice, and called on the blessing of his Dajbog, and promised him many gifts, but all in vain! This Žarko did not want to come! Not to me… may the gods see that he never go to his own mother either!"

It was then that Žarko finally revealed to her who he was: "Do not curse me so, my sister, for standing before you now is Žarko, your blood brother!" And the girl, when she heard this, jumped and hugged him round the neck: "Oh, Žarko, my dear blood-brother, do not let me be given to that blackest barbarian!" The hero stood up to assure her: "My Hur sister! While my head is on my shoulders, I will not let you be given to the barbarian; do not speak to anyone of me, other than the king and queen – have someone prepare me dinner and have it sent straight to the city inn. And do not skimp on the wine! When the wedding party arrives, have someone wait on them gracefully, and someone to cater to the barbarian so that he does not a pick fight while there in the castle. I already know where I will intercept the wedding party, if the gods grant me luck!" After this, they took leave of each other, Žarko heading for the inn, and the maiden to the king's castle.

A gentleman's dinner soon arrived at the inn, along with plenty of red wine. Žarko sat down to eat and drink his wine, while the city began to close up outside; when the innkeeper went to close the door of the tavern, Žarko asked him: "Why is everything shutting down so early?" The tavernkeep told him the real reason in a quiet voice: "Well, unknown warrior, the black barbarian has asked the king for his daughter's hand in marriage, and tonight he is to come for the girl; everyone fears him, so we are closing up early." But Žarko would not allow the door to be closed – he wanted to see this barbarian on this evening and all the so-called finery of the wedding assembly.

Soon could be heard the sound of horse hooves clopping through Leđan… And here was the barbarian on his horse in front, and trailing behind him more than two hundred wedding guests. Under the reins of the barbaric groom, the mare thrashed about violently, scattering stones in all directions from its pounding hooves, damaging houses and shops. When the party was in front of the inn, the barbarian mocked loudly: "I will be damned, but look at this wonder! All of Leđan is closed tightly, except the door of a city tavern! Is there no one in the inn, or are there those so crazy and gone that they do not know to fear me?" And turning dismissively, he continued on with his wedding party and went on to the king's castle to sleep there for the night. In the morning the king led out the barbarian's bride, along with twelve wagons of women's finery and garments, and the barbarian and his party marched back through the city with the maiden.

When passing once more along the same inn, they again noticed that the door of the tavern remained open, while all the other shops were still closed up. The barbarian this time could not resist having a look, and so pulled his horse over to see who could be inside. And there, sitting all by himself in the middle of the tavern, was Žarko, looking straight ahead and drinking wine; he was not drinking from a goblet, but rather from a pitcher large enough for twelve. And he did not lower his gaze even in front of the barbarian! The man then returned to his wedding party, wondering over this strange warrior. He failed to see how Žarko slowly rose from his seat, throwing on his wolf's cloak capped with the wolf's head. He then fitted his horse, not failing to clasp on his full wineskin on one side and his heavy mace on the other, and then took his battle spear in hand. Finally, he jumped up upon the horse and spurred it to rush through Leđan, hurrying after the wedding party.

He caught up to them in front of the city, and immediately began to stir up a fight. He was upsetting the entire procession, because the rear started frantically escaping forward as the uninvited guest pushed his way up front among them! As he spurred his horse towards the maiden, this strange outlandish warrior suddenly pulled out his sharpened sword from its sheath, and in two swings cut down the barbarian's best man and groomsman, giving them no chance to prepare.

The voice of these unfortunate events finally reached the bridegroom himself, as deserters of the party screamed in all directions: "Bad luck has come to you, barbarian – a warrior-hero has appeared at your wedding party! And this one is not as other warriors; he wears the cloak of a wolf, and on his head's crown sits the beast's own head, and something black is in his teeth, like a lamb of half a year! When he burst into the column, turmoil ensued, and he pushed right through to the front and struck down both your best man and groomsman!"

The enraged barbarian had the feeling that he had seen this warrior before, so he spurred his mare back, bounding up in front of Žarko at full speed and shouting: "Your bad luck is here, doomed man! What madness has sent you riding into my wedding party to slay my best man and groomsman? Are you drunk and mad from wine, or do you just hate life? You have angered me beyond the measure of your silly head… mark my words, as I pull the reins – first I will jump over you, then I will cut your head right off!" But Žarko was ready for such words: "Each word a lie, barbarian! Even with the Battle-god's luck, you shall neither pass nor reach me, let alone you leap over me!" And you should have seen the black barbarian! He tugged hard at the reins and drove his horse forward, truly meaning to jump over his opponent, but Žarko would not have it: he raised his own horse up on its hind legs to greet the charging mare.

Has anyone ever witnessed such a clash of warrior against warrior: the barbarian up against our Žarko! He could not vanquish Žarko, but nor would he allow himself to be defeated! The battle of brandishing swords raged and raged, as they pushed one another this way, and that, it is said, for four hours! Finally, it dawned on the groom that staying there could very well spell his end, so he suddenly spun his horse and fled through the gates of Leđan. Žarko hurried after him, but the barbarian's mare dashed more swiftly, like a spirit of the wind! The barbarian looked as if he would succeed in escaping, when Žarko remembered his mace: he swung it around and then hurled it powerfully forward, striking the barbarian in the shoulder. He fell from the impact, and Žarko quickly jumped down on him, cutting off his black head!"

All of those present and listening, even the exhausted Mara and Senka who had less reason for interest, stared fixedly at the storyteller who had paused for a moment to catch his breath.

"Žarko then took his opponent's horse by the reins and stepped through the gates of Leđan, but no one from the wedding party remained in the field. All alone stood only a beautiful young maiden, and around her twelve wagons of finery. Žarko went to his blood-sister, escorted her to the castle gates, then turned his horse around and spurred it right back to the city of Prilip.

While he slept the next morning, the king prepared six wagons of riches, and the girl her golden dagger, with the handle as a coiled asp, the raised head of the snake holding a precious stone in its fangs. We have all seen it, I think so. She also prepared and sent along the magnificent sabre with three hilts, inlaid with three precious jewels, among which was emblazoned the king's seal – by which not even a vizier could lay a hand on Žarko without first consulting the king! All of this was dispatched to Žarko in Prilip, alongside a letter from the king, which read: *May God bless you, hero Žarko, if you ever lack for riches, come again to your godfather!* And so, that is how the story goes as I heard it, and you can decide for yourselves whether there is truth in it or not. As it is said by the people, Žarko is known for this deed in two kingdoms: for he, from the lands of the Hurs, rose to great renown in Karavlaška, as this maiden eventually went on to enter into a royal marriage there, where she is now the queen. While the king of the Hurs, as you may well know, in the years ahead was blessed with two sons alongside his daughter, and the state has grown greatly in power, so that now, and for quite some time already, there is no question as to who will be the next to take the throne."

It was a bit strange to listen to this story of a legendary hero while that same warrior intermittently broke the trance of the tale with his loud snores and fits of turning about in his dreams, the rest of the company glancing over now and again at him: had they not seen him in action, it would be hard to believe that this was the same person, but now, after their night's battle, it seemed very possible indeed.

– Chapter 23 –
Shepherds Camp Shelter

Miloš now began examining the saber in even greater detail and with increased respect gazed on the exquisite blade which Žarko had bestowed upon him. As for the whole party, excepting, of course, Žarko, the remainder of the night was spent in a great deal of chatter and very little sleep, while Senka wondered repeatedly over all that had happened while she was away. Especially as she herself could not contribute to the incredible accounts, for her own strange experiences had to remain secret. They only drifted off to sleep just before dawn, when Miloš literally ordered them to get some rest. But, as it seemed to Senka, just as soon as they had lain down by the fire, Žarko woke them all up with his thunderous voice: "Get up, my victorious party, on your feet! Morning is here, time to get going!" Someone, it seemed, had slept quite well for the second half of the night, even if the time around midnight had passed quite differently. And he was now more than eager to finally get out of this confounding forest.

And indeed they managed to make it out of the forest in the evening of that same day. Not much happened along the way – Žarko and Miloš dictated the tempo, and the fast pace was not disagreeable to Senka and Vuk, nor to Mara, who now sat on Miloš's new horse, likely in recognition for all that she had contributed during the previous night. Brado and Vukan were again at the rear and showed no signs of difficulty in following the column. Žarko had wanted to know exactly what happened with Senka, but she was saved from further interrogation by Miloš and Mara, who related her lie from late last night in a much more convincing fashion than she was able to do the first time around.

Žarko's initial good mood grew worse with each new step they made, and so passed much like the day – slowly, but surely. While he was not happy to be trudging again, and had begun to grumble as before, he was still determined to leave "this damn forest," as he dubbed it, by day's end. This did not stop him from cursing through his whiskers more than once as they went. Shortly before reaching the forest's edge, Brado and Vukan brought the column to a halt: "Leader, we cannot go any further," they announced to Vuk. And Senka thought, and not for the first time, that the most incredible thing of all so far had been this immense shift in Vuk's stature; in just a few hours of her absence, the cripple had transformed from Žarko's servant and slave to the leader of a mystical tribe. She could not imagine what they were shapeshifting into, as it was difficult for her to believe in it; but she also dismissed the possibility that others were untruthful with her, so she simply chose not to think about the matter further.

"Go, my brothers, and may your steps go lightly. I will return to you as soon as I have the opportunity – expect me and wait for me." The newfound authority in Vuk's voice was mesmerizing. And so that was how they separated, quickly and without many words or emotions, as the two barefoot men simply retreated, fading into the forest behind them. However, just a few moments later, they heard Brado's voice. He called out for them to wait, then again approached Vuk, this time carrying across one arm some short pants and a vest in the exact same style as the ones he wore himself. "Vukan sends you these, my leader, for you two are built similarly. He says we will make new ones from our hunt last night, so these will serve you well. That which you've been wearing so far no longer suits you." Vuk smiled graciously and accepted the gift. Truly, the rags which he wore could hardly still be called clothes. Brado then turned and disappeared into the woods again, and the now shortened column of companions set themselves back on the path which led to the forest's border.

And finally, they emerged from the woods. It appeared that Miloš knew exactly where he was leading them and why: it was already beginning to grow dark when they passed the last line of trees and found themselves on what looked like a real, even foot-worn path. He immediately pointed out a shape just a bit off in the distance. "Over there, my companions, is a safe place. Here my shepherds bring their sheep before leading them through the forest, and also when they return from it." And now, truly, they could make out these shapes as two tents set on a clearing. Just sitting so, without anyone occupying them, they were simply waiting for any shepherds to show up. Apparently, apart from them, hardly anyone passed this way.

When they arrived a short while later at this camp where they intended to stay the night, they realized that there was nothing special to the place. The tents themselves were completely empty, made from the coarsest and cheapest fibers, wound roughly around a base of cut branches. Žarko frowned straightaway, wondering if such a setup could even keep them dry in the event of rain. In between the two opposing entrances of the tents, set just a few steps apart from one another and covered with the same crude fabric knotted to the same basic cuttings of wood, there was a small area encircled by stones where the shepherds would make their fires and some old cauldron turned upside down, probably so that the rain would not fall inside, nor on the ashes of the fireplace. Except for some occasional old footprints on the earth around the tents, there was no sign of anyone having camped there recently. "Another godforsaken hole," mumbled Žarko through his mustache, though not completely ill-tempered. After days enduring the impenetrable gloom of the thick forest, the place seemed relatively charming, and so with a new sense of optimism and energy, the entire party began to prepare for a night of camping out of the woods. Vuk again took upon himself the task of hunting down some meat, first changing into his new attire in one of the tents before setting out; the new garments fit him well, and he indeed looked like he was one of the men of Morlak, except for his limp. Miloš again furtively watched him as he approached the forest's threshold, trying to see the first steps of that strange transformation, but too quickly Vuk faded into the dusk, so the shepherd chieftain set to gathering as much wood for the fire as possible. Žarko, likely just for the sake of appearing willing to contribute, offered to help with the gathering, but without discussion resigned himself to the task of getting the fire started using the small branches being brought in or already there. His brother in arms saw that the man's grumbling had at least momentarily ceased, and he hoped it might stay that way with such an easy task. Even Marena involved herself in the preparations, turning the cauldron about and looking inside, then announcing that this night they would eat stew for dinner; she invited Senka to join her in gathering herbs and other greens from the fields around. "It would not hurt you to get to know which plants are edible, little one; I know that you cannot see them, but something tells me that you will recognize them well enough by smell."

Not a full hour later, they were all seated around the fire, listening as the dry branches crackled and flared while a meat stew simmered just above. Beside the fire, awaiting a space for roasting, lay skewers with chunks of the remaining meat of the wild goat which Vuk had nonchalantly carried out of the woods, as if there was nothing easier that hunting down this wary animal at dusk. For the soup they used the greater part of the remaining water from Miloš's flask, for he told them that close by a small creek flowed, at which they would all fill up their flasks the next day. The chieftain entertained them with stories of his life amongst his fellow shepherds, joking and cheerful, and all of them laughed heartily, finally unafraid of any danger in the vicinity. All the while Žarko was drawing large gulps of wine from his wine bladder, and soon he was joined in this by the other men, so that the happy company sometimes laughed at the stories even in places where they were not meant to be funny. And Senka laughed and laughed, feeling quite like as she once did, in that life that was no more in a home which no longer existed, on the occasion of a big holiday: unconcerned and joyful – for the first time since she had seen that smoke in the distance. She enjoyed every moment of this precious feeling, wishing that the evening would never end.

When, at last, it was agreed that it was time for sleep, Miloš suggested they divide the tents so that the men would sleep in one and the women in another. But Žarko, now completely flushed with wine, did not agree: "Not that way, my brother, the women must be watched over so that no wolves take them away. So instead, you watch over the little sister, you and Vuk, and I will deal with Mara, so that she cannot trouble me during the night!" And with that, Žarko raised himself up, somewhat shakily, while the others laughed, then he scowled comically, addressing the young woman: "All right, Mara, in my tent, so that I may watch over you and punish you for that from last night!" he said crudely under his voice, suppressing under his mustache the smile that her sonorous feminine laughter was inviting him to, taking her by the hand and leading her off right to where he said.

Sometime later, tucked into one corner of the tent, hugging Vidra and trying to fall asleep while Vuk and Miloš were both already breathing deeply, now and again snorting in their dreams, Senka could not get rid of the feeling that the said punishment was perhaps too much – Mara had groaned so much, even if this was muffled, that Senka was left asking herself what Žarko could be doing to her, drunk as he was. It could not be that he was hitting her or scolding her, as those sounds would wake the others… She then thought of something more, but quickly pushed aside such thoughts and turned away on her side, covering her ear with her hand and pressing as hard as she could. Just as she used to do when she would hear her father and stepmother during the long nights in the now burnt down house.

She still felt safe and sound for the first time in many days and hoped that this was just the first of many such nights. She could not even imagine how the very next day would change everything again.

Author's Note: If you enjoyed this book, please consider leaving a short review on Goodreads[4] and your favorite store (choose)[5] to spread the word – even a few words can mean a lot and help tremendously!

And if you want me to notify you when my next book is published, I invite you to join the infrequent Newsletter at my Website: follow the direct link to Book Two in my *Tale of Tales* series,[6] where you can shop signed books, subscribe via email (info)[7], find animated covers, excerpts, and more, including purchase links to all my vendors and titles. (Books on pre-sale are 50% off and can be read on a pre-release date if purchased directly from my website![8])

---

[4] www.goodreads.com/NikolaStefan
[5] www.NikolaStefan.com/choose-your-store
[6] www.NikolaStefan.com/book/Tale-of-Tales-part-2
[7] www.NikolaStefan.com/info
[8] www.NikolaStefan.com/Shop

THE NEXT BOOK IN THE SERIES:

Tale of Tales – Part II – The Witch-borne Quests

Being brave is not about being without fear, but mastering that fear. And in the company of heroes, even the most modest of souls may become one.

A TALE OF ANCESTRY EXCLUSIVE FOR THE PACK:

For Whom the Soul Tolls – A Story of Dark Heritage

A captivating personal fantasy story for the newsletter followers available only on the author's website. Learn how the then-young writer discovered his strange and frightening heritage many years ago…